STORNOWAY PRIMARY

WESTERN ISLES LIBRARIES

Readers are requested to take great care of the books while in their possession, and to point out any defects that they may notice in them to the Librarian.
This book is issued for a period of twenty-one days and should be returned on or before the latest date stamped below, but an extension of the period of loan may be granted when desired.

DATE OF RETURN	DATE OF RETURN	DATE OF RETURN
. . . .	. . . .	. . . .
. . . .	. . . .	. . . .
. . . .	. . . .	. . . .
. . . .	. . . .	. . . .
. . . .	. . . .	. . . .
. . . .	. . . .	. . . .
. . . .	. . . .	. . . .
. . . .	. . . .	. . . .
. . . .	. . . .	. . . .
. . . .	. . . .	. . . .
. . . .	. . . .	. . . .
. . . .	. . . .	. . . .

KT-161-931

GO TELL IT TO MRS GOLIGHTLY

CATHERINE COOKSON

GO TELL IT TO MRS GOLIGHTLY

DOUBLEDAY
London · New York · Toronto · Sydney · Auckland

TRANSWORLD PUBLISHERS LTD
61-63 Uxbridge Road, London W5 5SA

TRANSWORLD PUBLISHERS (AUSTRALIA) PTY LTD
15-23 Helles Avenue, Moorebank, NSW 2170

TRANSWORLD PUBLISHERS (NZ) LTD
Cnr Moselle and Waipareira Aves,
Henderson, Auckland

DOUBLEDAY CANADA LTD
105 Bond Street, Toronto, Ontario M5B 1Y3

Originally published in Great Britain in 1976 by
Macdonald and Jane's Publishing Group Ltd.
Corgi paperback edition published 1989

Published 1991 by Doubleday
a division of Transworld Publishers Ltd

British Library Cataloguing in Publication Data
Cookson, Catherine, *1906-*
        Go tell it to Mrs Golightly.
        1. English fiction
        I. Title
        823.914

ISBN 0-385-40136-1

Printed in Great Britain
by Biddles Ltd, Guildford and King's Lynn.

For Katie and Timothy Anderson –
two small bright sparks

1

'The Newcastle train's late. It's four minutes past two.'

'Aye, and at ten past two it'll be ten minutes late.'

'Don't give me any of your old buck, Bill MacKay.'

'And don't think you can get one over on me with your high-handedness, Joe Dodd. This is my province; I'm stationmaster here.'

'Huh! Stationmaster.' The tall man with the grizzled beard sprouting from his thin cheeks and chin again repeated the single word 'Huh!' which seemingly had the effect of infuriating the stationmaster, for he began to march up and down the short platform of the junction, pulling at the hard peak of his cap until it almost covered his eyes. All the while Joseph Dodd watched him, and every now and again he muttered to himself, 'Stationmaster!' And when his glance swept over the small booking hall and waiting room, then the beds of wallflowers just coming into bloom at each end of the platform, he added the word, 'Dogsbody!'

It wasn't until the signal indicated the approach of the two o'clock train at fifteen minutes past two that the stationmaster stopped his prancing and, casting a triumphant glance towards Mr Joseph Dodd, bobbed his head in one significant nod, as might a conjurer who had brought a rabbit out of a hat. He followed this by pushing the peak of his cap upwards and marching towards the man he had known for forty years and still didn't like, and said boldly, 'I pity any child, good, bad, or indifferent, who is unlucky enough to be put into your care, Joe Dodd.'

Joseph Dodd stared down at the stationmaster. A red blush spread up through his whiskers, over his brow, and into the white hair showing beneath his soft felt hat, and he demanded with a growl, 'Who told you I was meeting any child?'

"Tis common knowledge. You think that because you hide yourself away in that hole in the hill the village doesn't know your every move. You're a fool, Joe Dodd, always have been, a stubborn, big-headed, pig-headed old fool. No wonder your son couldn't abide you . . . Don't your dare!' The stationmaster took two quick steps backwards; then realizing he was almost balancing over the edge of the platform, he took another two steps sidewards and stood panting for a moment before turning and hurrying towards the end of the platform as if to greet the oncoming train.

Joseph Dodd, his arms hanging by his sides, slowly unclenched the fist of his right hand. Bill MacKay had been asking to be hit for years and one of these days he would do it. Yes, by God, he assured himself he would! Neither MacKay nor the villagers would have known anything about the child coming if it hadn't been for that Lottie Cassidy in the post office, her with the only telephone for miles. They had said they'd put a kiosk up after the war. Well, it was 1954 now and there was still no sign of one.

8

The steam from the train blinded him, its noise seemed to burst his eardrums, and the two together intensified the agitation within him. Why had he agreed to this? It was madness. Just for a month, those in Newcastle had said; but there were thirty-one days in a month and thirty-one days was a long time. The child was bright, the voice on the phone had said, and quite normal ... Why had they said that? They were holding something back. He had felt it from the first. Was she a cripple? he had asked. No, the voice had said, she wasn't a cripple. It had said something that sounded like handicap, then had ceased abruptly.

There were a number of people emerging from the steam. One was a boy, but he knew who that was – Harry Thompson's son, John, a fourteen-year-old, home from school. He hoped he found his father sober. And there was Parson Tempest's wife, sour Susan, with her daughter Jane. There wasn't much to choose between the looks of them. He glared at the mother and daughter. He hated women, all women, all females. And here were another two of them coming towards him out of the steam, a grown-up one and a young one. He didn't recognize the grown-up one; she wasn't the one who had come to see him after that phone call, for she had seemed to be as thick as a plank of wood and he could get nothing out of her. But the child this young woman was holding by the hand, he knew for a certainty, was his granddaughter, for if his son, David, had been born again and as a girl-child, she would be walking towards him now.

'Are you Mr Dodd?'

'Yes, I'm Mr Dodd.'

He didn't look at the young woman as he answered her for his eyes were now riveted on the

9

child, whose face was turned up to his. The eyes were wide and dark brown, but the lids were unblinking.

As he continued to stare at the eyes he experienced a very odd sensation: he wanted to recoil from them, from her. He had the desire to turn and run, to do anything to get away from those eyes, for he knew even before the young woman indicated to him by pointing to her own eyes that this child, his granddaughter, was blind.

'Hello. You're there.' Bella Dodd put out her hand and her fingers at first lightly touched the bottom of the old man's jacket. It was a rough jacket, thicker than the hessian she worked with at school; it had little nodules on it. Tweed. Yes, that's what it was, tweed. She knew her grandfather was tall; Miss Talbot had told her so and that he had a beard. Miss Talbot had told her she had to be very polite to him, especially at first, and not chatter too much until she found her way around. She was good at finding her way around; in fact, Mrs Golightly said there was none better at finding their way around. Mrs Golightly said that she had eyes in her brains, and that was better than having them stuck in front of your face, because most people who had them there never saw anything . . . He hadn't answered her. 'Hello,' she said again.

'What is this?'

Bella knew her granda wasn't talking to her but to Miss Braithwaite, and now she heard Miss Braithwaite say, 'Perhaps, if you . . . you could take us straight to your home, I . . . I could explain.'

Did Miss Braithwaite sound frightened?

She knew that her granda hadn't moved and

she sensed that he was now staring at Miss Braithwaite. After he turned about, Miss Braithwaite tugged at her hand and she walked with her.

There was a nice smell all about them, flowers ... wallflowers, just like they had in the school garden. She loved the smell of wallflowers. It filled her nose and she sucked it up right into her head and kept it there for a long time. She could keep things in her head, like smells, and the feel of cloth, and wood, and stone, and people's skin. Oh yes, she could keep the feel of people's skin in her head for a long, long time.

'Get up!' Her granda's voice was very rough. She didn't know if she was going to like it or not ... like him or not ... Oh! She gasped as she felt Miss Braithwaite's hands under her arms pushing her upwards. She thrust out her own hands to grasp at something and found they were gripping the rough material of the coat again.

'Gee-up there!'

Oh, they were being pulled by a horse; his hooves were clop-clopping and she could smell him. He smelled like cows, only different. 'Ooh! Ooh!' She laughed as she swayed, and she turned to Miss Braithwaite and asked, 'Is this a carriage we're driving in?'

'No.' Miss Braithwaite's voice really did sound frightened. 'It's a cart, a flat cart with sides, and we're sitting on a seat that runs along the front.'

'Oh, I like it. Have you many horses, Granda?' She turned her body to the side, but the next moment Miss Braithwaite had tugged it straight again and was whispering in her ear, 'Don't talk.' Yet after giving this order she herself went on talking, but Bella could scarcely make out what

11

she was saying above the rattle of the cart.

'We . . . we are passing through the village. It's a very nice place, small but very nice. There's a general shop on the right of us and some cottages and an inn; then a blacksmith's shop.' She paused here before saying, 'To the left is a rather large house, next to the church. It'll be the vicarage.' There was another pause before she added, 'There's a group of cottages down in a hollow. I suppose they are where the farm workers live.'

After a longer pause Miss Braithwaite spoke again. 'We are now in the open country, Bella,' she said. 'To the left are well-cultivated fields, and beyond them is a farmstead; and beyond that the hills rise upwards. But on the right-hand side of us the hills are much nearer.'

There was a long, long pause now and Bella felt she would like to say something, anything. She just wanted to hear herself talking. She couldn't talk to Gip – well, not here because people were funny about Gip. They didn't seem to understand him. But Miss Braithwaite had started again.

'Oh, this is interesting, Bella. There's a big house lying away to the right of us. It is turreted and there's a long drive leading up to it. We're passing the gates now, but it's all very over-grown. I don't think anyone can live there.' Now Miss Braithwaite raised her voice as she leaned in front of Bella and asked tentatively, 'Does anyone live in that house, Mr Dodd?'

'Stop your jabbering, woman. You've never ceased since you got off that train.'

There was a silence bereft of human voices now that hurt Bella, and it had evidently hurt Miss Braithwaite, because when she did speak again her voice trembled. She said, 'It is necessary, Mr

12

Dodd, that I explain . . . I mean, point out the surroundings to Bella.'

'Nothing is necessary. You're wasting your time.'

Now only the clop-clop of the horse's hooves, the swishing of its tail, the flapping of the reins, the jingle of the harness, the grinding of the cart wheels, the sudden wafting of a bird as it winged its way above their heads, the lowing of cattle in the distance, a train whistling far, far away, and the thumping of her own heart filled the void deprived of the human voice and told her that this new grandfather of hers didn't like her. She had said to Mrs Golightly, 'What if he doesn't take to me?' and Mrs Golightly had laughed and said, 'Never you fear, he'll take to you all right. But if he's a bit sticky at first, it'll be up to you to work on him. Talk to him, tell him about things. And remember what I've always told you: if you are afeared of anything, tackle it. The only way to get over fear is to face it.'

'I'm very good at washing up, Granda, and I can knit and make straw baskets and mats. I can also play tunes on the piano. I'm very good at that . . .'

She felt she was going to be lifted wholly from the cart and into the air, the way Miss Braithwaite jerked at her arm; then she was made aware that the cart was turning and the wheels were going over cobbles. She was also aware that the light had changed, that the brightness had gone from the day.

The cart stopped and Miss Braithwaite lifted her to the ground. Then they both stood, Miss Braithwaite watching and Bella listening, as Joseph Dodd took his horse and flat cart towards the stables.

13

'Where are we, Miss Braithwaite? Has the sun gone in?' Her voice was a whisper now.

'No, dear, it's only that the house is built almost –' She paused and Bella knew that she was looking about her, before she went on, 'It's built right onto the hillside. I . . . I shouldn't think it gets the sun all day.'

'Is it a nice-looking house?'

'Yes . . . yes, quite nice. It's like a large cottage . . . oh, bigger than a cottage. It's on two floors and has what looks like an attic above. It could be very pretty with flowers about.'

'Aren't there any flowers, Miss Braithwaite?'

'No, no, I'm afraid not.'

'Are we in a yard?'

Again there was a pause before Miss Braithwaite spoke, and then she said, 'Yes. Yes, it's quite a large yard, cobbled. Your grandfather's work seems to be connected with wood. There's a lot of thin trees piled up at the end of what appears to be a stable block, and there's a saw bench and other things near.' She paused again before she said, 'They look like willow trees. Shh! Your grandfather's coming back.'

Bella heard her grandfather approach; she felt him pass her quite close. She heard a key being turned in a lock. She thought it was an old key and an old lock because the sound was heavy and grating.

'Come.' Miss Braithwaite's voice was low and her hand, as it gripped Bella's, trembled slightly, then it actually jerked Bella's hand upwards as her grandfather's voice boomed now.

'Look at it, woman! Look at it! How's she going to find her way around in here? The first thing that'll happen is she'll break her neck.'

14

'She's ... she's very good at finding her way around once she's been directed.'

'But who's going to look after her, clothe her ...?'

'I can clothe meself, dress meself, and I can put the kettle on an' make tea, an' make toast, an' peel taties. I can light the stove and put the pan on. I've done it for me da comin' home. Mrs Golightly said I was a dab hand at it.'

'Well, we've got no stove here, miss; it's a coal fire.'

'Well, I can learn once I'm shown, and Mrs Golightly said ...'

'Shut up!'

'Don't shout at me!'

Following this retort there was a silence, and Bella knew that her granda was staring at her, and she knew from the pressure of Miss Braithwaite's fingers just how he was staring at her.

'Leave her there a moment and come outside, you.'

Her granda's voice was no longer shouting but it now had a kind of finality about it that made her body slump. When Miss Braithwaite directed her to a chair, she sat in it and, as she would have said herself, went all flop.

Her granda and Miss Braithwaite were now in the yard and, she imagined, some distance away, but she could still hear most of what they were saying, for as Mrs Golightly had often told her she had ears as big as cuddy's lugs.

'You hoodwinked me.'

'I did nothing of the sort.'

'Well, the other one did.'

'Miss Talbot did it with the best of intentions.

15

She thought if you saw the child you could not help but like her . . . and pity her situation. I have only been dealing with the case for a week since Miss Talbot went into hospital, but she told me that Bella is very sensitive and is a lonely child because her father kept her to himself. He apparently did his best. He took her to school in the mornings and one of the teachers brought her back home at night, but she was often alone in their flat for hours. Your son, perhaps you know, was a lorry driver and his working hours were erratic. What is more, the child spent a traumatic weekend alone. Her father failed to come home, and when she knew he was dead she didn't speak for days, and as you may have already noticed she's a ready talker. When it was discovered after some long delay that the child had a grandparent, you were advised of your son's death . . .'

'My son died for me when he left here fifteen years ago.'

'That's as may be, Mr Dodd, but officially your son died six weeks ago, and . . . and because he had left no information concerning any relative it took some time to discover you . . .'

'And from that you thought you'd better go warily, that's about it, isn't it, before you panged a blind child on me.'

'It wasn't like that at all. The school Bella's been at till now is a day school; she couldn't be left alone during the Easter holidays. The alternative was to send her into a home, but Miss Talbot and the Committee thought that before they took this decision they would contact you. And Miss Talbot did so, and you offered to take the child during the holidays. After that, she's to go to a boarding school.'

'Aye, aye, I did, but I've been hoodwinked. Your Miss Talbot must have thought I was blind too, and, by God, I have been! I thought she was dim, but what she was . . . was wily . . . Women!'

Bella, her body straight now, her ear turned in the direction of the door, waited for the silence to pass. Then her grandfather's voice came to her again, saying, 'How long has she been like that?'

'Her eyes were weak from when she was born, so I understand. Her mother was very young, only sixteen. She had to take the child to the hospital every week, and it must have become too much of a strain for her because she left the child and her husband before the child's first birthday. I don't know all the ins and outs of the case. I'm merely acting as guide today because of Miss Talbot's sudden illness. But I understand your son apparently did his best for the child. He wouldn't allow her to be taken into care; he even went to court once in order to keep the custody of her. They tell me that when Bella was five she could see relatively well, but then she contracted measles and other childhood ailments and these weakened her system. Her sight went completely when she was six years old.'

'The sins of the fathers.'

'Well, you should know about that, Mr Dodd.'

'Look you here, miss! Don't you come that with me. I've lived a blameless life. I've been a God-fearing man all me days, and I brought me son up . . .'

'To fear his maker; and you, too, I should imagine.'

Bella had pulled herself to the edge of the chair; her toes were touching the ground, her body was stiff. Eeh! Miss Braithwaite must have stopped

17

being afraid of him for now she was giving him what for. What would he do to her? Hit her?

'For two pins I'd send you and her packing.'

'Well, that's what you intended to do from the beginning, isn't it, Mr Dodd? But I can tell you that I, too, have come to a decision: I intend to take her back because I can see you are not the right person to look after her. She'd be happier in a home . . . far happier.'

Bella moved quickly from the chair. Her hands outstretched, she began to walk towards the stream of fresh air, which meant the doorway, and when she reached it she groped around and stood for a moment before shouting out, 'Please!'

She knew they were both looking at her and waiting for her to go on. She knew what she wanted to say; it was all in her head and in her chest. There was a great feeling in her chest, a painful feeling. She had had it there since they told her her father was dead. She thought they had meant he was dead drunk, as he so often was, but then they had explained to her that he was dead dead, and from then she knew that she was alone, except for Gip and Mrs Golightly. But neither of them could make up for her da. And then two weeks ago she had heard she had a granda and the pain in her chest had sunk right down. But now it was back again and it was stopping her from speaking.

She put her hands out and walked towards where she imagined they were standing, and when Miss Braithwaite's voice said gently, 'Bella,' she turned her body to the right, then stopped. What she said now was simply, 'I don't want to go back, Miss Braithwaite. I want to stay with me granda.'

She was lost in the silence until the horse neighed. After that her granda spoke. 'Show her the ropes inside,' he said. 'I'm going to see to the animal.'

Bella held out her hand but Miss Braithwaite did not take it immediately. When she did, she gripped it and almost took Bella at a run back into the house.

'Now!' Miss Braithwaite's voice had an excited sound. Bella could feel the excitement going right through her, and she said in a whisper, 'What is it like, Miss Braithwaite?'

'Cluttered, but very homely. Now we'll start. You come in through the door and right opposite to it is the fireplace; but mind, there is a table in the middle. Take four steps. Now here we are at the table. Come round it to the right. That's it. Now here is a big wooden chair, likely your grandfather's.'

Bella felt the arms of the chair and placed her fingers over the pad on its seat, and then Miss Braithwaite said, 'You can feel the heat of the fire. Now you're standing directly in front of it. Put your foot out and you'll touch the steel fender. That's it. Now let's see. The length of the fender will take four of your steps. Try it. There, I thought so. Now at this end you can lean over and touch the side hob. There's a pan standing on it. Can you feel it?'

'Yes, Miss Braithwaite, and I could easily take it off.'

'I . . . I wouldn't do that. It might be full of liquid, boiling liquid. And remember you mustn't do anything that is going to hurt you or cause trouble with . . . with your grandfather.'

'What is at the other side of the fireplace?'

19

'An oven, a round oven. I've never seen one like it before but I'm sure it's the kind that makes lovely bread.'

Bella knew that Miss Braithwaite was smiling; the smile was coming over in her voice.

'Back to the table we go. There are two wooden chairs under it. Can you feel them? So far, so good. But now we come to the clutter. I would keep clear of this part of the room if I were you. Go no further than the horsehair sofa.'

Bella placed her hands along the seat of the sofa, then with a touch of laughter in her voice she said, 'It's prickly.'

There was laughter in Miss Braithwaite's voice, too, as she replied, 'It's a very old sofa and the horse, I am afraid, is pushing its hairs out all over it.'

For the first time since Miss Braithwaite had met the child, she now heard her laugh outright. After a moment she took the child's hand again and said, 'When you want to go up the stairs, make for the sofa; the stair post is right opposite. Up we go!'

Together they mounted the bare oak stairs, counting as they went. 'Eight, nine, ten, eleven, twelve.'

'Here we are then. Oh, the landing is quite straightforward. There are just three doors going off it. Let's see what is behind the first one.'

'Oh, my goodness!' Miss Braithwaite's voice had dropped to a whisper. 'That is your grand-father's room, the big bear.' She laughed again, then went on, 'And what's behind this door? Oh, this I imagine has been got ready for you.'

'So he meant to have me, Miss Braithwaite. If he got the room ready he must have meant to have me, didn't he?'

20

'Er . . . yes. Yes, I should imagine so.'

'Where's the window, Miss Braithwaite?'

'It's here. But it's quite small, and I don't think it has been opened for a long time. And here is your bed, to the side of it.'

'Has it got curtains on it, Miss Braithwaite, the window?'

Miss Braithwaite looked at the curtains, which must once have been blue but which now appeared a washed-out grey, and she said, 'Yes, feel them.'

'What colour are they?'

'A pretty blue. They match the patchwork quilt on your bed.'

'And . . . and the floor, what colour is the floor?'

'Oh.' Miss Braithwaite paused as she looked down at the linoleum, which had evidently been washed so often it was almost devoid of pattern, and she lied boldly as she said, 'Well, it's a kind of yellow, a golden yellow, you know. It has flowers on it and it matches the wall-paper.'

'Oh, it must look pretty.'

'Come.' Miss Braithwaite felt she couldn't lie anymore at the moment and she led Bella towards the door. But she stopped as she went to go out, saying, 'Oh, I forgot. Come over here. There's a chest for you to put your clothes in. It has five drawers and is just a little taller than you. Feel it.'

'It's got big wooden knobs on it.'

'Yes, it has big wooden knobs.'

When Miss Braithwaite opened the third door on the landing, she exclaimed, 'Oh, this is just a lumber room. There are odd pieces of furniture and boxes in it.'

'And apples.'

'Apples?'

'Yes, I can smell apples.'

21

'Oh, very likely. Yes, very likely it's been a storeroom. Those boxes could have been for apples. Perhaps there's an orchard somewhere about. Come along.'

'Will you show me where the washing-up is done? There must be a kitchen.'

'Yes, yes, of course. I've forgotten about that. There must be a kitchen.'

In the living room again, Miss Braithwaite looked about her, then exclaimed, 'Oh, there's a door at the far end; it's beyond the wooden chair. It's a good thing it's at the clear end of the room.'

A few seconds later Miss Braithwaite was standing in the stone-floored scullery and gazing about her in dismay. A shallow stone sink was attached to one wall of the room, and under it was an old bucket, and on the small table to the side of the sink were some tin mugs and two tin plates. Opposite the sink and placed in the corner between two walls was set an old-fashioned wash boiler, and next to it was an equally old-fashioned mangle.

'Is it a nice kitchen?'

'... Very ... er ... pleasant. A bit old-fashioned but very serviceable. Here is the sink ... and here is the pump. I think you can just reach it.'

'A pump?'

'Yes, feel it. It likely pumps the water up from a well.'

'Will I be able to drink it?'

'Yes, yes, of course ... Come.'

Bella felt her hands tugged away from the round scaliness of the pump and Miss Braithwaite was saying, 'Here's the door that leads directly into the yard. It's on the side of the

22

house, but from just outside where we are standing now you can take in the whole yard, because the cottage . . . the house appears to be long and narrow. Ah! There's your grandfather.'

They were walking across the yard now and Bella knew that her grandfather was not approaching them, but she became aware of him as she neared him because of the smell of his clothes. They had a smoky smell, like that which had come from her father's clothes, except that this was a stronger smell. Men who smoked baccy instead of cigarettes had this smell about them. But her grandfather's clothes also had a woody smell, a sawdusty smell. She was well acquainted with the smell of sawdust because they passed a saw mill on their way to school.

'I like your house, Granda.'

When there was no immediate answer to this, she added, 'It's a very fine house; and I love my bedroom and all the colours in it.' She lifted her face upwards and turned it first in one direction and then the other, aware that the adults weren't looking at her, but at each other.

'I must be going now. You'll drive me back to the station I hope, Mr Dodd?'

'Wh . . . what? Drive you back to . . .?'

It was either the sound of protest in her grandfather's voice or the fact that she was aware that Miss Braithwaite was about to leave without being offered some hospitality that caused her to put in, 'But you've never had a drop of tea or anything, Miss Braithwaite. Mrs Golightly always used to say, if you were from next door or far away it costs very little to offer a drop of tay.'

'Oh, Bella!'

She knew Miss Braithwaite was smiling

23

broadly, but it was towards her granda she turned when he demanded, 'Who's Mrs Golightly?'

'She's a grand woman. Me da said she knew all the answers. She was kind, nice.'

'Who was she?' Her grandfather was now addressing Miss Braithwaite, and Miss Braithwaite replied, 'I don't know. I never met any neighbour of that name. But then, as I've said, I've only come new to this case. Miss Talbot would likely be able to give you further information.'

'Well, shall we have a sup of tea, Granda?'

Without waiting for an answer, she now went on, 'I bet I can find me way straight to the back door ... Come on, Gip! Come on.' She now slapped her small side twice, half turned, then held out her hand before hitching away towards the side of the house.

Joseph Dodd watched her, his lower jaw sagging, his eyes screwed up to slits; then, turning his head slowly towards Miss Braithwaite, he said, 'Gip? What now, Gip?'

'It's her imaginary dog.'

'An imaginary ...? The same as this Mrs Golightly?'

'Yes, I suppose so. Motherless children always make up companions, both human and animal. They have to have something.'

Joseph Dodd turned his head towards where Bella was standing, her arms outstretched triumphantly in the opening of the back door. He gazed at her for some seconds before looking at Miss Braithwaite again and demanding with a growl, 'What in the name of God have you landed me with, woman?'

24

2

'Eat your porridge,' he said.

'It's very thick.'

'There's milk to your . . . your left hand.'

'Oh.' Bella put her hand out and touched the jug, saying, 'It's nice and round and smooth. What colour is it?'

'. . . Brown.'

'It's warm.'

'It's dead cold. It's been in the pantry all night.'

Bella gave a little giggle now and said, 'I mean the colour.'

'Warm?'

'Yes. My teacher said all browns are warm.'

'Get on with your breakfast.'

'There's a lot of salt in it.'

'There should be a lot of salt in it – it's porridge. And don't dawdle. I've got to go on an errand.'

'Oh, are we going on the cart?'

'I'm not taking the cart. I'm going over the hills.'

'May I come with you?'

'It's too far. You'll have to stay here and not wander. Do you hear that? Not wander.'

'Yes, Granda.' Her voice was flat; then on a higher tone she added, 'Haven't you got a dog, Granda?'

She heard the scraping of his chair on the stone floor. She heard him go towards the fire and the water being poured into the teapot, and when he again returned to the table and didn't speak, she asked, 'Don't you like dogs?'

'My dog died a short while ago.'

'Oh, I'm sorry, Granda. It's awful to be without a dog. I couldn't be without Gip.'

When her granda's spoon clattered against the tin plate she asked, 'Are you going to get another one?'

'Yes, when it's old enough to leave its mother.'

Her voice rose to a squeak as she cried, 'Oh! That'll be wonderful, Granda. A dog! Is it a missis or a mister? What colour is it? What are you going to call it?'

'Finish your breakfast, child. I've got to be on me way and I want you outside to show you how far you can go.'

Her voice had dropped from its heights when she answered, 'Yes, Granda.'

Five minutes later they were standing outside the front door and he was talking. 'Right opposite here there's a gate; don't go beyond that. You know your way to the back door and if you turn to the right from there, you make a dead line for the stable. But don't move beyond that to the right because there's me saw block, and there's stacks all about. But come along an' I'll show you where you can go for a walk to stretch your legs.'

When Bella held out her hand towards him he did not take it; instead, after a moment's pause he said, 'Hang on to me coat.' She groped towards him, and having found the bottom of his jacket, she gripped it. When he moved forward she hurried by his side until he came to a stop.

26

'Here we are fronting the stable door,' he said. 'Now turn your body half round to the left and feel the wall with your right hand. Now here's where it ends. Then there's an open space. It's a narrow piece of field. Now keeping in a straight line, walk across it like this. Come.'

Again she was hurrying by his side, and as of habit she counted her short steps. Twenty-five of them.

Now he had stopped again, and he was saying, 'This is me piece of woodland. There's an opening here to it in the hedge. Can you feel it?'

'Yes, Granda.'

'Now from this post I've put some ropes along the path. I've attached them to trees and they go right to the boundary. There, put your hand on this one.'

He didn't direct her groping hand, but she found the rope and smiled up at him and said, 'I've got it, Granda.'

'Well, leave loose of me coat now and keep your hand on it and come along.'

She traced her fingers along the rope until she came to a tree, when she put both her arms around it and said, 'I like trees.'

'Never mind about that. Follow the rope.' His voice was a growl.

She followed the ropes attached to four more trees before coming to an abrupt stop by a wall. He hadn't told her about the wall and she almost bounced back onto her bottom. There was just the slightest trace of tears in her voice as she said, 'You ... you never told me about the wall, Granda. I could have bumped me head.'

'I didn't tell you because I wanted you to find it out for yourself; and that wall is important.

27

You don't go beyond there. That's me boundary.'

'It's broken, the wall.'

'I know that, but it's their job to fix it. None of them, though, ever stay long enough to do anything. Rack and ruin the place has gone to. Whist! ... whist!'

She became quiet and still as the sound of footsteps on gravel came to them. When they had faded away, she turned to him and said, 'There's a path quite near.'

'It's the drive to the house. It curves here onto the front of the house.'

'Are there flowers beyond there, Granda?'

'Flowers?' He didn't reply for a moment, then said, 'Yes, yes. Daffodils.'

'I could smell them. Why don't you have flowers, Granda?'

'No time for flowers.'

She knew he had turned about so she turned too and, gripping the rope again, followed him as he said, 'Never go beyond that wall. Do you hear?'

'Yes, Granda.'

'This is a grassy path. It's about ... well, six foot wide.' He turned towards her. 'Step it out.'

She left the rope, turned, and had taken seven steps when his voice checked her, saying, 'That's enough. The willows start from there. Don't go in among them. There's damp patches, boggy ... You know what boggy is?'

'No, Granda.'

'Well, it's wet ground and you can sink into it.'

'Very far?' Her voice rose to a question mark.

'Not very far, but far enough, especially where the springs are. Anyway, you keep out, you understand?'

'Yes, Granda.'

28

'Come on with you, back. I've got to be on me way.'

'How long will you be, Granda?'

'I don't know. An hour, two; it all depends.'

'Well, I'll wash the breakfast things and tidy up before I come out to play.'

'You'll do no such thing.'

'I will so! I can. I know me way about; Miss Braithwaite showed me; and Mrs Golightly said I'm better occupied. She said there's more people die of boredom than overwork, and what's more . . .'

'Be quiet!'

'I was just sayin'.'

They reached the yard in silence. It wasn't until they were opposite the stables that Bella spoke again. 'Can I go in and stroke the horse?'

'No, you can't. Do you want to be kicked in the teeth? Have sense, child.'

'Ironsides never kicked me in the teeth.'

'Ironsides?'

'Yes, I ride on Ironsides sometimes. He's lovely. His skin's hard and soft and he smells nice and . . .'

'Child!'

She became still, her hands hanging by her sides, her face turned up towards him, waiting.

She heard him gulp in his throat, the palms of his hands rubbing together, and his heavy boots scraping on the stones before he spoke again. Then he said, 'This has got to stop. An imaginary dog, a Mrs Golightly, and now a horse. Do you hear me, child? This has got to stop!'

'But they're not 'maginary, at least . . . well, not all. Mrs Go . . .'

'Stop it! I say. You've got to forget about Mrs Golightly.'

He was saying she had to forget about Mrs Golightly who was the comfort of her life. She stretched up her face towards him; then she gave way to what her teacher said was her main failing and one that she must endeavour to overcome, because people didn't love a defiant child. But she wasn't in school, she was in this new place where everything was strange to her, and if she couldn't talk about Gip and Mrs Golightly, then she would cry. And she knew from experience that if she started to cry, she wouldn't be able to stop. They'd had to get a doctor to her the last time she had a crying bout. She was in bed for days afterwards, and she didn't like staying in bed; the time stretched to twice its length when you stayed in bed. So now she forgot whom she was talking to and her voice almost matched his shout as she yelled up at him, 'I'm gonna talk to them. I've got to talk to somebody and they're my friends. And Miss Talbot said it was all right to talk to them, and I could keep them as long as I needed them . . . I mean, Gip. And I could talk of Mrs Golightly and Ironsides when . . .'

'Be quiet!'

'I'll not.'

'What did you say?'

'I said I'll not be quiet. I've got to talk. I must talk to somebody; if I don't I'll cry.' Now her head was bobbing at him as she ended, 'And mind, if I cry you'll know about it 'cos I can't stop once I start cryin'. They threw water in my face once but still I couldn't stop.'

The silence spread around her again and no sound came to her to break it, not even of bird song or of the horse's hooves on the cobbled

30

stable floor behind her, until she said in a small voice, 'Are you mad?'

Again there was a silence before he answered, 'Yes, I'm mad.'

'Well, you've only got yourself to blame. If you'd only let me talk to you. I . . . I wouldn't talk all the time. I . . . I can be quiet for ages. I was always quiet in the mornings when my dad had a bad head, especially on Sunday mornings . . . Where are you going?'

The footsteps stopped and she knew that he hadn't turned to her as he said, 'I told you, I'm going over the hills. I won't be long. I've put the guard round the fire; don't go near it. And if it should rain, get into the house and sit quiet until I come back.'

She made no response but stood where she was until she could no longer hear his footsteps, then she put out her hand and began to walk towards the back door. But as she neared it she stopped, stood still for a moment, then, jumping around, she patted her hip twice and cried, 'Come on, Gip!' and, with her hands outstretched again, she made for the stables.

After reaching the stable wall she ran along by it until she came into the open space, and then, her hands outstretched, she ran onto the grass and towards the opening in the hedge. But here her direction went astray and as she moved along the hedge towards the right she said, 'Is it this way, Gip?' After three or four steps she answered herself, saying, 'No, it's the other way, silly.'

When she came to the opening she gave a little laugh; then going through it, she grabbed at the rope, at the same time crying, 'Come on! Come on! I'll race you to the wall.'

31

'Oooh!' When she bumped into the tree she put her free hand to her head, saying, 'Why didn't you tell me it was there? If you don't do your job right, I'll leave you back in your kennel. Yes, I will.' She nodded down towards the ground. Then stooping, she made a movement with her hand, saying, 'I was only fooling. I wouldn't lock you up, never, never. No, I would never lock you up, Gip.'

When she reached the wall she leaned against it, panting and sniffing. 'Can you smell them? There must be hundreds of them. And there's narcissi there, 'cos I can sniff them a mile off.'

She was moving along the wall now, and when her hands groped at the air and she fell forward over the stones strewn about her feet she said, 'Oh, dear me! It must have all tumbled down here, Gip. What a pity I can't go across and pick some flowers.'

She straightened up, her hand searching for the wall again. When she found it, she was about to walk to where the rope was attached when she heard footsteps on the gravel that her grandfather said fronted the big house. She moved quickly back towards the tumbled stones and the gap, telling herself that if the people walking there could see her they might come across and talk to her.

The footsteps were passing her now. Whoever was walking there must surely see her, that is if there wasn't a hedge bordering the drive. Her granda had said nothing about a hedge, but then she hadn't asked him, had she?

The footsteps faded away and she turned reluctantly and groped along the wall until she reached the rope. She was halfway along the grass path towards the yard when she remembered she

32

hadn't called Gip, and so, turning, she patted her hip twice and called, 'Gip! Gip! Come along! I'm going indoors to wash the dishes. Come on now!'

She waited a moment, then heaved a sigh and said, 'That's a good boy,' then continued slowly down the path and into the yard and across it to the kitchen.

She had been here three days and she hadn't talked to anyone except her granda. She kept talking to him but he didn't talk much back. And she hadn't touched anyone since Miss Braithwaite had left. Her granda hadn't touched her. And she had wanted to touch him; she wanted to feel his face for she didn't know really what he looked like except what Miss Braithwaite had told her. But that wasn't the same as how he would look if she could feel his face.

She had been in bed now a long time but she couldn't sleep. She had cuddled Angela, her doll, but the china face had brought her no comfort. The house was very quiet except when her grandfather broke the silence with a snort. Outside, too, there was no sound. The birds were all asleep. There had been a scuffling noise once or twice in the yard; she had heard it on the other nights too. Her granda said it was a fox, which generally went across the yard on his nightly prowl. It was making for Harry Thompson's hen coop down the road. Her granda didn't seem to like Harry Thompson very much because he had said it would serve him right if the fox collared all his hens; it might sober him up. From this she gathered that Harry Thompson took a drop . . . Her granda didn't seem to take a drop, ever. The only thing she smelled off her granda's breath was onions.

33

When she heard him snort again, an idea came into her head. He was sound asleep; why didn't she go in and feel his face now? He'd never know, because Mrs Golightly said she had a touch like thistledown . . . when she liked.

As she got out of bed and went to move towards the door, a light hit her eyeballs and she turned towards the window. The moon must be shining. She was still able to distinguish between night and day and she knew it was far from daylight yet.

Softly she lifted the latch of the door and as softly, her hands outstretched, she made for the opposite door. When it began to creak as she opened it, she remained still for a moment; then, holding her breath, she squeezed herself through the aperture.

She knew where his bed was – she had gone into his room and fingered around unknown to him – and now she made straight for the foot of it. When her hand touched the iron rail, she paused a minute before walking up by the side of the bed. Then putting her hand out, her fingers really as light as thistledown, she felt the outline of her grandfather's shoulder. He was lying on his back; that was likely why he was snoring. Her dad always snored and snorted when he lay on his back. Now her fingers were touching the beard on his chin. Softly they moved upwards until they were only a skin's breadth away from his lips. A fly would not have left a deeper imprint than her first and second fingers as they traced the outline of hair covering his mouth. And now she was touching his nose. It was a thin nose but very long. Her fingers moved onto his cheek. There was a hollow here but his cheekbones were high, right under his eyes.

Joseph Dodd dropped his lids over his eyes, shutting out their startled, almost hypnotized stare only just in time, but her fingers on his eyeballs caused his stiff body to jerk, and he knew that the hand had been lifted but was still hovering above his face.

When he felt her touch skimming over his thinning hair he could stand no more. He coughed, spluttered, then turned onto his side, and he didn't seem to breathe again until he heard the door creak; then it seemed to him that his body had fallen through the feather mattress, so deeply did he sink into it. It was some minutes later when he said to himself, 'Something will have to be done.'

Across the landing, Bella was hugging Angela again and talking to her softly. 'His face is hairy, very hairy,' she said; 'except for his nose and eyes, and his forehead, of course, and that goes a long way up. He has no hair on the front of it. He must be old, very old. How old was my dad? Thirty-six. Then granda must be twice that old, mustn't he? Or nearly, anyway.'

The last thing she said to Angela before sleep overtook her was, 'I don't think I like the hair around his mouth. I think it would get in the way if he were to kiss me. But then I don't think he'll ever kiss me, will he, Angela? No, no, you're right. I don't think he ever will.'

3

'Get your coat on. We're going out.'

'For a ride, Granda?'

'No, not for a ride, for a walk.'

'Where to?'

'You'll find out soon enough.'

He was grumpy this morning, she could tell by his voice. And she could picture his face, all the hairs on it bristling. Perhaps he was out of sorts; perhaps he had a headache.

'Have you got a headache, Granda?'

'No, I've got no headache. I don't drink so I don't have headaches.'

Oh, that would have been one in the eye for her dad, 'cos he always had headaches after a booze up.

A few minutes later they were both outside standing near the gate leading into the road. 'We're turning right here,' he said. 'The road is straight for some way, half a mile or so, then it divides into two. We're taking the left-hand branch that goes towards the coast.'

'Where the ships are?'

'No, there's just the bare coastline and cliffs. But we're not heading for there; we're going to see a man called Harry Thompson.'

'Oh! That's where the fox gets the chickens?'

As he came to an abrupt stop, she bumped into the back of his leg and had to steady herself against it for a moment while he said, 'You repeat nothing that ɪ say about him or his chickens, you understand?'

'Yes, Granda.'

'I'm going to ask him a favour, the first I've ever asked of any man in me life, and it'll be as much as I can do to keep me temper with him, so don't you aggravate me with your chatter.'

They were walking on again, she holding on to the end of his coat, and it took a great effort on her part to stop herself dancing in front of him when she heard from quite near the barking of a dog. Then it seemed to be only the next minute that the dog came to them, and as it was running in and out between her and her granda she caught hold of it. She buried her hands in its long hair, and when its tongue came right across her face she let out a high gurgle of laughter and fell onto her knees beside it, only to be brought abruptly to her feet, not by her grandfather's hands but by his voice, shouting, 'Get up out of that!'

'Hello there.' It was a strange voice speaking. It could have been a nice voice but it sounded gruff, sort of on its guard, and what it said bore this out. 'Well, Mr Dodd, this is a surprise. What can I do for you this fine day?'

It was some seconds before her grandfather answered, and then he said, 'I've come to ask you a favour, Harry Thompson.'

'My! My! Joe Dodd asking a favour of Harry Thompson. Wonders will never cease.'

'I'm not askin' it for meself. I never ask anyone for anything, you know that.'

'Oh yes, I know that. Well, if you're not asking

37

for yourself, who are you asking it for?'

'Oh.'

Bella knew that her grandfather must have indicated her by a nod or a look; and now he was addressing her, saying, 'You stay put, Bella, stay beside the dog. I'll be back in a minute.'

She heard the two sets of footsteps walking some distance away and she stopped fondling the dog in order that she could hear what they were saying. When they stopped walking she distinctly heard her grandfather say, 'She's blind, stone blind. I've got her on me hands for a month until she goes back to school. But she's lonely, she wants some contact with young 'uns. I'm here to ask if you would let her come and play with your son?'

'Play . . .? Play with John? But my boy's past playing; he's fourteen gone.'

'I didn't mean play in that way, not ring-a-ring-a-roses. She's not that kind of a child anyway.'

'How old is she?'

'She's coming up nine by years, so they tell me, but she's nineteen in her head, or older; and she's got a tongue that would cut old rags, never stops. All I'm askin' is that he should take her for a walk now and again over the hills, or as far as the coast, and then she might get rid of her imaginary friends.'

'Imaginary friends?'

'Aye. She's got a dog called Gip, and a horse called Ironsides, and an old wife that she alludes to as Mrs Golightly.'

When the peal of laughter reached Bella she bit on her lip and buried her head in the dog's ruff. Her granda was making her out to be crazy not right in the head, like Mary Kinton. Mary was

38

blind, too, but she threw herself about and laughed at nothing.

They were walking towards her now and the man was saying, 'Well, I'll put it to him, but you know what lads are, especially at his age. In the meantime I'll take her round and show her the animals, if it's all the same to you, Mr . . . Dodd.'

There was still that defensive sarcastic note in the man's voice and Bella was surprised at her grandfather's reply, for his voice was quiet as he said, 'I'm obliged to you.'

'Hello there, little girl.'

Her hand was taken from the dog's neck and held firmly, and she looked up at the speaker and said, 'Hello, mister.'

'My name's Thompson, Harry Thompson.'

'Hello, Mr Thompson.'

'Would you like to go round the holding and see the animals? Not that we have many, but they're the kind that pay their way.'

The last words were turned from her and she felt that the man was again looking at her grandfather; and now her granda said, 'I'll be off then. When will I come back for her?'

'Oh, don't bother. One of us will bring her along.'

Bella knew that her grandfather was standing over her now and his voice came down at her, quiet and deep, saying, 'Behave yourself. Don't make a nuisance of yourself. And check that tongue of yours if you can.'

'Yes, Granda.'

The man, too, must have stood watching her granda walk away into the distance because it was some time before he turned her about, saying, 'Well now, what would you like to do first? Find my boy or look round the place?'

39

'What's his name, Mr Thompson – your boy, I mean?'

'John.'

'Is he a big boy?'

'Yes, he's tall for his age, fourteen.'

'Oh!' She remained quiet for a moment. 'If he doesn't want to talk to me it doesn't matter. I'd just as soon talk to you and see the animals.'

Again the man's laugh rang out, and now she joined hers to it. Then he said, 'You know, I feel we have something in common, you and me – we like to talk. But there's my John. Now, by a strange quirk of character he's not unlike your grandfather – he doesn't have much to say for himself, quiet type he is.' When his voice faded away into a personal mutter, she was just able to catch the words, 'And there might be a reason for that too,' before he said aloud, 'He's down in the bottom field. We have a few sheep, just a dozen or so, and he's gone to see to the lamb. It's one I had to bottle feed; the mother wouldn't own it. Now none of them will own it and it's having a rough time of it, poor thing.'

'Is this a farm, Mr Thompson?'

'No, no, my dear, nothing so glorified, just a small holding: a few sheep, some ducks, hens, rabbits, a few geese. We did think of having a couple of cows but then' – there was a pause – 'cows need regular attention, like women and children; you need to be there all the time.'

'And are you not here all the time?'

Mr Thompson now made a sound like a chuckle, but she termed it a sad chuckle because he said, 'Yes, I'm here all the time, and then again, no, I'm not here all the time. Ah! Here he is. Come on, up you go!'

She felt herself lifted high up in the air, then dropped at the other side of a gate. Once again he was holding her hand and running with her now, calling, 'John! John!' When they had stopped running he said, 'I've brought someone to see you.'

There was no response to this remark, and now Mr Thompson cried, 'You'll never believe who's visited me – Mr Joseph Dodd himself! He brought his granddaughter.'

Bella felt her hand lifted upwards. 'He was wondering if you and she could have a little chat now and again.'

Bella knew that the boy in front of them was about to make some remark. She also knew from the movement of the fingers grasping her hand that Mr Thompson was signalling to his son. Finally he said, 'This is Bella Dodd, John.'

Bella held out her hand, and after a moment it was taken, given a small shake, and a voice said, 'Hello.'

She answered it, saying, 'Hello,' then added, 'Has the lamb taken to its mother?'

'No.'

'Oh, that's a pity, 'cos it'll be very lonely.'

She felt Mr Thompson's hand jerk away from hers, and now she was standing alone. No one spoke for a moment until the boy said, 'I'll bring the lamb.'

When he brought it he pressed it against her knees and she put her hands on it, then went down on her haunches. Her arms about its wriggling body, she cried joyfully, 'Oh, it's lovely! Lovely. Cuddly. What do they call it?'

'Call it? Nothing, just lamb.'

'Oh, I'd call it Woolly because it feels like the wool I knit with. I can knit. Do you know that? I

41

can knit. I sometimes drop the stitches but not half as many as the rest do. And the wool feels just like this.'

'I'd let it go now.'

'All right. Yes.' She stood up, then the boy said to her, 'Stay where you are a moment; my father wants me.'

She heard him moving across the grass, then Mr Thompson's voice so low that she couldn't make out what he was saying, but she heard his son's reply quite distinctly. 'But she's only a child, a bairn. What'll I do with her?'

Now Mr Thompson's voice came to her, saying, 'Just once or twice a week for an hour or so. He must have been at his wit's end to come to me, you must admit that.'

'But she's a girl.'

Harry Thompson gave a small laugh now as he said, 'Yes, that's evident enough. And she's a bonny one in the bargain. It's a pity unto God that she's handicapped as she is. But she's cheerful, I'll say that for her, as bright as a button. There'd be no need to pity that one, because she doesn't pity herself.'

'But what can I do with her? Why didn't he go into the village? There're girls there.'

'It's four miles away and who is there there between five and sixteen except the parson's snooty piece, Miss Jane. I can't see her offering to do a good deed for the day by taking the child around. Now if it was you she was going to take around, she'd jump at the chance.'

'Oh, Dad!'

'Never mind "oh, Dad!" '

'Well, you know I can't stand her, or any girl for that matter.'

42

'Well, this one isn't a girl, she's just a child coming up nine.'

'She seems ready enough with her tongue.'

'Oh aye, that seems to be the trouble, so our respected neighbour Joseph says. He tells me she's got an imaginary family, a dog called Gip, a horse called Ironsides . . .'

'What!'

'As I said, a dog called Gip, a horse called Ironsides, and an old woman named Mrs Golightly.'

'Is she barmy?'

'Well, judge for yourself. Did she sound it? No, no, boy; she's not barmy. But she's lonely.' His voice dropped to a whisper now. 'Old Joe's a hard old stick and his son must have had a devil of a time with him, else why did he scamper off and leave him? By what I could gather from Bill MacKay, and what he gleaned from the young lady who brought the child here a few days ago, the child was left by her mother when she was but a year old and David apparently brought her up himself. If the child is near nine her father must have been twenty-seven or so when she was born, so he couldn't have married for some years after he had left here. Anyway, just think what it must be like to have a bright spirit like that child has and not be able to express it through your eyes.'

To Bella's strained ears there now came a very strange ending to the conversation of which she had only been able to gather snatches, for the boy asked, 'Are you going to the village tonight?' and when after a pause his father replied, 'No,' the boy said, 'Very well, I'll take her out then.'

It had been a wonderful week, at least in parts; if only her granda had talked to her or taken her hand, she couldn't have asked for anything more. But anyway, it had still been wonderful because John had taken her out twice; once up some hills, and when she'd got to the top, her hat had blown off and he'd had to run down after it. When he had returned with it she couldn't thank him for laughing. She had gone on laughing even after he had said he couldn't see anything funny about it. He was a bit grumpy, was John, not all the time, just now and again. His father wasn't grumpy. Oh no! Mr Thompson was a lovely man. She liked him very, very much. Mr Thompson was kind – she could tell by his voice that he was kind – but somehow she didn't think that John thought he was kind. John spoke to his father funny at times, harsh. John reminded her of someone, she couldn't quite remember who. Anyway, he was going to take her to the sea today. It was all of three miles away, John said, that was by road, but he was going to take a shortcut over the hills. She'd have to tie her hat on with a bow under her chin. She gave a little giggle at the thought, but it was cut off abruptly by her grandfather's saying, 'Don't laugh when there's nothing to laugh about, child.'

'I had something to laugh about, Granda. I . . . I was seeing meself with me hat tied on with a piece of string and in a bow under me chin.'

'I can see nothing funny in that.'

'Mrs Golightly used to say . . .'

'I don't want to hear anything more of what Mrs Golightly used to say.'

'You're in a bad temper today.'

'I'm in no bad temper but I've got work to do. And you keep yourself out of mischief until that boy comes for you.'

44

'He's not coming until two o'clock and it's only just struck one. I could help gather up the strips of bark. The long strips feel just like the pieces we have for making the wickerwork baskets. The teacher, he says they come from oysters.'

'Oysters? Nonsense! What you mean is osiers. Oysters are fish.'

'Well, that's what the wickerwork comes from.'

'Don't be silly, child. Osiers are willows, willow trees.'

'Well, anyway, we learned about them . . . about willows and how they make paper from them, and dye, and he said some are used for medicine.'

'Nonsense!'

'It isn't nonsense, Granda, he read it out to us. He said oysters . . .'

'*Osiers.*'

'Oh well, he told us there were all sorts and sizes. Some grow higher than houses and some so little you can hardly see them.'

'He's talkin' rot.'

'I think he was a clever man; Miss Talbot said he was. I once made a little basket for Mrs Golightly and she said whoever taught me to do that was a man in a thousand. She said . . .'

The door banged.

Oh, her granda was a bad-tempered man. He couldn't stand the sound of Mrs Golightly and she herself couldn't help talking about her. Well, why should she? Mrs Golightly had been with her as long as Gip, and she had understood all about Gip . . . What was that? There were voices in the yard. Had John come early? She groped her way to the door and opened it. Then pulling it wide, she ran forward, crying, 'Miss Braithwaite! Miss Braithwaite!'

45

'Hello, my dear. How are you?'

'Oh, I'm lovely, Miss Braithwaite. I'm fine.'

'Are you enjoying your stay?'

'Oh, yes, yes!' She stopped and, sensing another presence, turned her head to the side. After a moment's pause, Miss Braithwaite said, 'This is . . . this is a friend of mine, a Mrs Campbell. She's coming for a holiday. She's renting a cottage just outside the village.'

'Hello, Mrs Campbell.' Bella extended her hand, but it was some seconds before it was taken, and then Mrs Campbell said, 'Hello. I . . . I understand they call you Bella?'

'Yes, but I don't like it very much. I like the name Joy. Mrs Golightly –' She bit on her lip and turned her head towards where she sensed her grandfather was standing, then said, 'Well, a lady I knew had learned a piece of poetry at school when she was a girl. She said it had a hundred and eighty-six verses but she only knew two of them. It was about a child called Harold or some such and it was about a dance. She used to laugh and jig as she said it:

On with the dance! let joy be unconfined;
No sleep till morn . . .

'I've forgotten the rest but she used to say that was me, joy unconfined, except . . .'

'Hold your tongue!'

She stopped herself only just in time from saying, 'I can't. I'll get me fingers wet,' because that's what they said to each other at school when the teacher told them to hold their tongue.

Now her grandfather was going for Miss Braithwaite: 'You weren't due until tomorrow and she's going out now!'

46

'Well, that's all right, Mr Dodd. Are you taking her for a ride?'

'No, I'm not! She's going with young Thompson to the coast.'

'Young Thompson?' There was a note of enquiry in Miss Braithwaite's voice. 'A boy?'

'Aye, a boy.'

'How old is he?'

'Fourteen or so, I should say. What does it matter?'

'I should think it matters a great deal! Are there no little girls . . .?'

'No, there are no little girls hereabouts, except in the village, and they're still in rompers. This boy is of good character. I'm a judge of character. He's got one fault but it isn't his – he happens to be the son of his father.'

Bella now heard the two visitors clear their throats; then Miss Braithwaite said, 'Well, we won't trouble you any further, Mr Dodd. Bella looks in good health; she's got roses in her cheeks and she seems to be enjoying her stay. Would you mind if we took her for a walk, perhaps along the road to meet this new friend of hers?'

'No, I've no objection. It'll save further talk, and an argument likely. Good day to you.'

When Bella heard her grandfather turn away she said, 'Tarrah, Granda.' There was a pause in his step but he made no reply; then Miss Braithwaite took hold of her hand, saying gently, 'Come along, Bella.'

At the gate Miss Braithwaite asked, 'From which way does your friend come?'

'Sometimes he comes by the road but sometimes he jumps Mr Pollock's gate. I go to meet him by myself now. I know the road, an' there's

47

no motorcars come this way, an' I always have time to get out of the way of a horse and cart. Look, I can walk in the middle of it and keep a straight line.'

She darted from them, and as she proceeded to demonstrate, she heard Miss Braithwaite say to her companion, 'Well, now you see what we're up against,' and the lady reply slowly, 'Yes. Yes, I do. I do indeed.'

She stopped and waited for them coming towards her, and when they were abreast of her she turned and held out both her hands to them, saying, 'We're near the gates of the big house, the one you told me about when you brought me, Miss Braithwaite. Remember?'

'Yes, yes, of course. It's a derelict house,' Miss Braithwaite now explained to her companion. 'A small country mansion. It's very overgrown . . .'

'Oh, it isn't that what you say,' Bella now put in, 'I mean derelict, because somebody lives there now.'

'Really!'

'Yes, the end of granda's wood isn't far from the top of their drive and I've heard the gentleman walking up the drive numbers of times. And yesterday I heard him talking. I heard what he said. He said he was expecting the minister to call, and he laughed about it.'

'You have very sharp ears, Bella.'

'Yes, yes I have, Miss Braithwaite.'

'Oh, oh' – Miss Braithwaite was speaking under her breath now – 'here's someone coming through the gates, a . . . a gentleman.'

Bella waited, her face turned to the side as the footsteps neared them. They were firm footsteps, hitting the ground hard, and when they came to a

48

halt in front of them and the gentleman spoke, saying, 'Good day, ladies,' she thought, He's got a nice voice but ... She didn't know why she added the 'but'. It was just a sort of odd feeling the voice gave her.

Both Miss Braithwaite and her friend answered together, 'Good day,' and the gentleman said, 'It's a beautiful one, isn't it? A day for walking.'

'Yes, indeed. Indeed.'

Bella knew that Miss Braithwaite was smiling.

'And who have we here? I think I recognize this young lady.'

'She ... she happens to be a neighbour of yours. She is Mr Dodd's granddaughter.'

'Oh, yes. Yes.' There was a pause now, and she knew that it was being filled with signs from Miss Braithwaite to the gentleman to indicate that she couldn't see him. She heard faint whispered words, which he cut off immediately, but which she recognized as 'How sad'. People always said that, how sad, and she wasn't sad, well, not all the time, like today when she could feel Miss Braithwaite's and the lady's hands holding hers, and very shortly John would hold her hand and even help her over gates and to jump ditches.

'Well, good day. I hope you enjoy your walk.'

The gentleman was moving away, and she joined her voice to Miss Braithwaite's and the lady's, saying, 'Good day.'

'What a nice man.' Miss Braithwaite sounded impressed.

'Is he big? Is he old?'

'Yes, he is big, tall, very tall.'

'Old?'

'No; about forty I should say, and very

handsome. Don't you think so, Mrs Campbell?'

It seemed to Bella strange that Miss Braithwaite should call her friend Mrs Campbell, and it was also strange that the friend didn't answer Miss Braithwaite straightaway. In fact, Miss Braithwaite had to repeat the question, and when Mrs Campbell replied it was as if she were just coming to out of sleep, or some such. It was like when she was at school and the teacher would say, 'You're not paying attention, wake up! Wake up! You're not paying attention.'

'Yes, yes, I suppose he was, but ... but a little over suave. I ... I can't see a man like that settling in the country.'

'No?'

'No.'

'Well, he seemingly has. And oh, here's another young man coming towards us.' She now wagged Bella's hand. 'It could be your companion.'

When the footsteps halted in front of them Bella said, 'Hello, John.' But, like her grandfather, John made no reply. It wasn't until Miss Braithwaite said, 'Hello there,' that he mumbled, 'Hello, miss.'

'I understand you and Bella have become friends.'

'Well ... I ... I take her around.'

'It's very kind of you. I ... I am Miss Braithwaite, and this is a friend of mine, Mrs Campbell. You'll likely be seeing much more of Mrs Campbell than of me because she's ... she's having a holiday here.'

'Oh ... I ... I hope you enjoy it. It's nice country.'

'Yes ... yes, it is, very nice country.'

Bella noted that Mrs Campbell's voice was soft

50

and had a kind of tremble in it as if she was afraid of something. Bella now held out her hand to John, and when after a moment's hesitation he took it, she turned to the ladies and said, 'Well, thank you for coming all this way to see me, Miss Braithwaite. Will you be coming next week too?'

'Yes, yes, I suppose so. I'll be visiting you until Miss Talbot can return to duty.'

'Is she still bad?'

'Yes, yes, she's been very ill. But in the meantime you'll be seeing quite a bit of Mrs Campbell because I'm sure she'll be taking walks along this road, won't you, Mrs Campbell?'

'Yes, yes, indeed. I . . . I like walking.'

'Oh, that'll be nice.'

'Well, we're going now. Bye-bye.'

'Bye-bye, Bella,' said Miss Braithwaite cheerfully; but the other lady just said, 'Bye-bye,' in a sad sort of way. Bella didn't know what to make of Mrs Campbell, not yet at any rate.

They were well out of earshot before John spoke, and then he said, 'You were bragging yesterday that you could walk the road by yourself, so why do you want to hang on to me?'

'I don't want to hang on to you. I just like holding your hand. Don't you like holding my hand?'

John made no direct reply to this but what he said now was, 'Going this way, we've got to pass the Pictons' cottage. They're a rough lot. They used to be charcoal burners; they still do a bit of it. Your grandfather supplies them with chips. If Gerry and Pat are about, they'll likely call and jibe.'

'Why?'

'Well, just because they're made that way.

51

They're tough. They always want to fight.'

'Can't we go any other way?'

'Yes, we could, but it would be too long for you to walk. This way cuts off nearly a mile and a half.'

'Is that why you don't want to hold my hand?'

He did not reply for some seconds, and then he muttered, 'It looks sissy. To anybody it looks sissy, but they'll make something more of it.'

'Oh.' Gently she withdrew her fingers from his grasp, and now he said immediately, in a contrite tone, 'It'll be all right. I'll keep one arm still and you can feel my sleeve.'

'How far is it to this place?'

'Oh, another ten minutes' walk or so.'

'We're going downhill now, aren't we?'

'Yes, but it levels out in a minute. Then the road runs straight to the cottages. There's a wood on one side and some banks on the other.'

'How far is it then to the sea?'

'Twenty minutes to half an hour; it all depends how we walk it.'

'It's a nice day. I . . . I feel I want to skip.'

'Well, don't, unless you want to break your neck. There's a ditch to the right of you and it's deep.'

'I can feel the sun on my eyes and I can see all coloured lights, beautiful coloured lights.'

His hand now pulled her to a stop. 'You can see coloured lights?'

'Yes.'

'You don't just see blanks?'

'No, no, like I told you, I can tell you when it's night or day or when the moon is shining.'

'But colour?'

'Well, I remember colours – black, white, blue,

green, yellow, pink, mauve. Why are you staring at me?'

'I . . . I was just thinking. Anyway, how do you know I'm staring at you? . . . Aw, come on.'

They had walked about a dozen steps when she heard him exclaim, 'Oh!' under his breath and the sound of the word made her ask, 'What is it?'

'It's . . . it's the Pictons. They're on the road.'

'Are they . . . are they not nice lads?'

'No, they're not nice lads. Keep close to me and keep walking.'

She kept walking, her head going from one side to the other the while, and she knew that they were nearing the boys before the rough voice came at them, saying, 'Ah, here's Gentleman John out for a walk with his lass. Cor! Can't you get one your own size?'

Sensing danger in the taunt, she put her hand out quickly and caught John's arm.

'Where you goin'?'

'That's my business.'

'Not so. 'Tis our business too. You're walkin' on our path.'

'It's a public road.'

'Who said so?'

'I said so.' Bella felt herself jerked to a stop and she was startled by the loudness of John's voice. She hadn't heard him raise his voice before. Now a different voice spoke and it came from the right of her. It had a sort of laughing gurgle in its tone when it said, 'Aw, let them be, our Gerry.'

'Who's touchin' 'em? . . . What's the matter with her? Gapin' like a stuffed pig.'

'Shut up, you!' It was the laughing voice again but not laughing very much now as it finished, 'That's old Dodd's kid, the blind 'un.'

Bella felt herself jerked forward and they were some way along the path when the rough voice came, crying, 'I'll get you some time on your own, fancy boy,' and Bella knew that John had half turned in the road as he cried back, 'Any time. Any time.'

It was a little while before she proffered a remark, and then she said, 'They're not nice.'

'Well, what do you expect? They live like wild animals out there.'

'If they had hit you, what would you have done?'

'What do you think? I would have hit them back.'

'Two to one?'

'Oh, be quiet! It's true what your grandfather says – you never stop talking.'

It was some moments before she said, 'That's the only way I can see people . . . and when I touch them.'

And it was some moments later, too, when he muttered, 'I'm sorry.'

She covered his embarrassment immediately by crying, 'Can we run?'

'Oh no, no!' He pulled her back. 'We're nearing the top of the cliff. Can't you feel the breeze?'

She stopped and sniffed and said, 'Yes, yes; but I thought you said it was flat near the sea.'

'Yes, it is once you get down onto the beach, but we've got to go some way along the top here before we can find a way down, and then it's pretty steep. That's why there's never many people here, because the going's so rough.'

A few minutes later he said to her, 'Now look, do as I say. There's a path cutting the side of the cliff and it's very steep, but you'll be all right if you do as I tell you. I'm going down backwards and I'll hold your hand, right?'

'Right.'

Only once did she lose her footing on the way down, and when he grabbed at her and pulled her back against the rock face he seemed to knock the wind out of her body for a moment. She stood gasping until he said, 'I'm sorry. I had to grab you like that else you would have gone over.'

'Was it my fault?'

'No, but the ledge narrows here. Anyway, we're nearly there.' When a few minutes later he said, 'Here we are!' she cried at him, 'Tell me what it's like.'

'Well, it's just a little bay. The sand here is dry but the tide's been turned some time and in another hour this will be covered with water.'

'Can I plodge?'

'Yes, I suppose so, if you want to.'

'Oh! I want to.'

When she sat down on the sand and lifted up her dress and pulled down the garter from below her knee, John turned away, shaking his head.

A minute later she was on her feet, crying, 'Come on! Have you got your shoes and socks off?'

'No.'

'Aren't you going to plodge?'

'No.'

'Aw, John! Aw, come on. I can't plodge on me own.'

He looked upwards. There was nobody walking along the top of the cliff there to see him; nevertheless he told himself that wading was a daft thing to do at his age.

Reluctantly he sat down and took off his shoes

55

and socks; then he was running with her towards
the sea.

When they emerged from the shelter of the
cove, the wind caught them and she cried, 'Oh,
me hat!'

'Take it off.'

Before he had finished speaking she had pulled
the elastic from under her chin and thrown the
hat behind her; then she squealed a high joyful
squeal as her toes touched the incoming wave.

For the next half hour she jumped and ran and
splashed the water up onto John, and he, forget-
ting his great age, splashed her back again. When
at last he called a halt and said, 'Come on, you've
had enough,' she went obediently with him. They
sat down under the shelter of the cliff and he
pressed something into her hand. Her fingers
moved around it and she said, 'What's this?'

'Chocolate.'

He almost fell over as she flung herself upon
him, her arms about his neck, crying, 'Oh, thank
you, John! Thank you. Oh! I'm so happy. Oh!
I've never been so happy. Isn't it a lovely day?
I've plodged before but never like that.'

'Give over! Let go!' He tried to disentangle
himself from her.

His face red with embarrassment, he finally
pushed her onto the sand again, but this
brusqueness in no way affected her talking. His
face grew even more red as she gabbled, 'Oh, I do
love you, John. Have you got a girl? Mr Jarvis –
you know, the basket teacher – he's got a girl, a
young lady he calls her. She's a teacher in a big
school and she sometimes comes and reads to us.
Dennis Bottomly – he's the one that can see a
bit – he said they hold hands. Well, that's

nothing, holding hands, is it? . . . But have you got a girl?'

'Don't be silly! Don't talk such rubbish.'

'I just asked you.' Her tone was less exuberant now.

'Well, you shouldn't ask questions like that. They embarrass people.'

'I'm sorry.' She sighed and, her voice now low, she said, 'Mrs Golightly used to check me about that – embarrassing people. She said it was because I couldn't see their faces. But she also said that, when I grew up, a prince would come along and whisk me away, and we'd be happy ever after, like in the stories. But I knew it was just a story and she was just saying it to comfort me so I would have something nice to think about when I was by meself and not feel so lonely. I know that no one will ever really want me, not off their own bat, they won't. They might be pressed into it like me granda was in taking me on for a month . . .'

'Don't be silly!' He cut in on her now. 'I never heard such rot. Where do you get those ideas from anyway? Of course somebody will want you, 'cos you're beautiful.'

In the silence that followed even the waves didn't seem to create any sound, but she knew that he had gotten to his feet, and she also knew in a way that he had embarrassed himself more than she had by what he had said.

Her voice was very quiet now as she muttered, 'You're not just saying that to please me?'

'. . . No, no, I'm not. Anybody'll tell you if you ask them.'

'Well, you can't ask people that, can you? I could have Mrs Golightly, but nobody else. What

57

does my face look like, John? Tell me, please . . . Please.'

'Well –' There was a long pause during which she knew that his eyes were on her, and she waited, her face turned up to his. Then he said haltingly, 'It's sort of round, yet your chin sticks out a bit; your nose is small, and . . . and your eyes are big and a lovely colour, brown; and your hair matches; and your skin is . . . well, it has a creamy texture, a thick creamy texture.'

'Oh' – she shook her head slowly and a smile spread across her face – 'I'm not bad then?'

'No.' He gave a small laugh as he added, 'No, you're not bad,' and he only just stopped himself from adding, 'But you're the strangest kid I've ever come across.' And yet in a way she wasn't so much of a kid. In some ways she had much more sense than that Nancy Cutter in the village who was always waylaying him, or any of those girls that hung about the schoolyard. They were all barmy. All girls were barmy. Except perhaps the headmaster's daughter. But she was old, eighteen or so, and they said she looked down her nose at even the head boy.

'We'd better be going now,' he said. 'Are your feet dry? Get your socks on; the tide's well up.'

A few minutes later, having donned his own shoes and socks, he watched her expertly buttoning her shoes, and he thought to himself, I went to town over her face; I could have just told her that she had a cherublike look. But then again she mightn't have understood what I meant; perhaps she hasn't heard the word cherub. But the more he looked at her now, the more he realized that that would have been an apt description of her, because her features were the same as those of the stone angel that hung out from the arch of the school chapel, and the look was emphasized by the eyes, wide, staring, sightless. He felt a wave of pity for her well up in him as he ended his thinking with, Poor kid . . .

Yet within the next hour he was to eliminate forever from his mind any resemblance that this 'poor kid' had to an angel . . .

Before they reached the Pictons' hamlet Bella's step began to slow. When he said, 'Come on, put a move on,' and she answered, 'I'm out of puff,' he stopped and, looking at her, exclaimed impatiently, 'Well, I told you it was a long way, didn't I?' Then he added, 'Wait a minute! Stay there.'

When he returned he put into her hand a thin but sturdy branch of a tree, saying, 'This is almost like a walking stick. See, it curves towards the top, and it's just your height.'

Bella laughed as she tried it out now, saying, 'Yes, yes, it is. Have you got one?'

'No.'

'Why didn't you get one for yourself while you were at it?'

'Because I don't need one. Come on!'

They passed the Pictons' cottage without being assailed by any voices and they were walking by the stone wall that ended above the ditch that bordered the road when abruptly from behind the wall two heads appeared. Bella was startled by the aggressive voice that she had heard previously, saying, 'You got back then from playin' pot pies?'

She waited for John's answer but he remained mute; and then the voice came again, 'How much an hour do you get for lookin' after her?'

59

'You mind your tongue, Gerry Picton, else I'll look after you.'

'You and who else?'

Bella was aware that they were being confronted by only one of the Picton boys, for another voice from some short distance away called, 'Leave them be, our Gerry.'

'I'll leave him be after I've closed his mouth.'

'Get by, out of the way.' Bella felt John pushing her to the side, and again he said, 'Go on, over the ditch. Keep clear.'

When he let loose of her, she knew she was standing on the edge of the ditch, and she could have jumped it with ease, but she didn't. The next minute she heard the first thud of a blow and the gasps and grunts, and she cried out, 'John! John!'

A voice near her said, 'It's all right, leave 'em be, let 'em fight it out.'

'No, no. Go and stop them. Go on, please, stop them.'

'Not me. Not me.' There was a gurgle in the boy's voice. 'Our Gerry would knock me brains out.' Then the boy's voice changing, she now heard him yell, 'Let him up, our Gerry! Let him up! 'Tain't fair.'

Bella now had a mental picture of John lying on the ground and the big bully of a Gerry standing on top of him. Without waiting to think, she rushed towards the spot from which the gasps and groans were coming, and taking the branch in both hands, she swung it with such force that it spun her around. As she went she heard a high-pitched yell that verged on a scream, and, her circle completed, she made for the place from which it came. Again she lashed out with the

60

branch, but downwards now, and again there was a yell, followed by, 'Keep her off me! She's barmy, mad. Keep her off me!'

When two hands gripped her and drew her backwards she knew it was John, and after he had pulled her over the ditch he commanded between gasps, 'Stay there, and give me that thing here.' But when he went to pull the branch from her hands she gripped it tightly, saying, 'No, I won't! They could start again.'

She heard him let out a long breath before turning away, and now she heard him speaking to the other boy, saying, 'Hadn't you better go and see to him? He's bleeding.'

And the voice answered, 'Aye. And so are you. You'll have a shiner the morrer.'

'But she hit him on the head with that branch.'

'Well, what are you makin' all the fuss about? He asked for it, didn't he? If she hadn't come in, he would likely have brained you. He never knows when to stop, our Gerry.'

'Aren't you going to see to him?'

'No, an' don't you go near him either, 'cos the way he's feelin' at this minute he'll likely kick your guts out. But the morrer he'll just be talk again. He's mostly all talk, but he doesn't like you, an' he had to have a go at you; but now you've stood up to him he'll leave you alone. He's like that.' There was a pause, and then the boy added, 'She's got spunk, the blind kid, hasn't she? I nearly laughed meself sick the way she went at him. You would have thought she could see him. Can she see a bit?'

'No.'

'Eeh! Well, she's got a good sense of direction, like a bloodhound . . . Your lip's bleeding. An' see who's coming along there – it's your father, and it looks as if he's three sheets in the wind. 'Tisn't your day, is it?'

John turned and looked along the road to where a man was zigzagging his way towards them. When he heard his father's voice burst into song he closed his eyes tightly for a moment. Only when he was drunk now did his father sing that ridiculous song. The words came to him now, adding to his humiliation: 'Touch the harp lightly, my pretty Louise.' He used to sing it in fun at one time. That was before his mother died. He hadn't drunk hardly at all then.

It wasn't yet five o'clock – he must have been indulging after closing time in the back room of The Bull and he had promised . . . But hadn't he promised before? John sighed and opened his eyes and saw his father waving his hand to him. As he approached nearer he stopped his singing and cried, 'Ah! What have we here? The gathering of the clans: my son and heir, and one Patrick Picton, and Joseph Dodd's ray of sunshine. Hello there, my dear.'

Bella knew that Mr Thompson was bending over her and that he was drunk, for his breath gave strong evidence of this. 'He stinks of whisky,' she said to herself. Her dad had given off a different smell, sometimes rum and sometimes beer, but Mr Thompson's smell was distinctly whisky. She said cheerfully, 'Hello, Mr Thompson.'

'Hello, me dear. And how are we today?'

'Oh, fine, Mr Thompson. We've been to the beach and we plodged and had a lovely time, but coming back one of the Pictons' – she flung her arms to the side – 'set on John, but he lathered him. And I went in with a stick too.'

'You did? Good for you. Good for you. Where is he, the Picton who dared to stand up to my lad?'

'Father, come on. Come on home.' John had now grabbed his father's arm as he made for the side of the road to look over the wall; and Harry Thompson, in what could have been termed a soothing tone, said, 'It's all right. It's all right, boy. I'm on me way home. I just wanna see who you lathered, 'cos that one is standin' on his feet.' He pointed to where the younger Picton was leaning against the wall, grinning.

'Come on, Father. Come on, do you hear?'

'All right. All right, me lord; here we go homeward bound. Take my hand, dear. Take my hand.' He held out his hand towards Bella, and when she groped for it and couldn't find it he lurched towards her, saying, 'Sorry, me dear. Sorry.' Then doing a kind of erratic hopping dance, he almost lifted her from her feet. But she went with him laughing as he now sang:

'Yip! I-addy-I-ay-I-ay,
Yip! I-addy-I-ay.
I don't care what becomes of me,
Long as I sing the sweet melody,
Yip! I-addy-I-ay-I-ay,
Yip! I-addy-I-ay.'

John followed behind. His eyes were cast towards the ground but he couldn't close his ears to his father's voice.

Then his shame deepened. As they approached their own gate, who should he see coming from the opposite direction but the lady he had seen accompanying Miss Braithwaite earlier on in the

63

day. She had stopped further along the road and she was watching their approach. When his father caught sight of her he stopped his singing. Then doffing his hat with an exaggerated flourish, he called to her, 'Good day, madam. Good day. Isn't it a splendid day for gettin' drunk?' Then without further ado he turned in to the gate, and the lady resumed her walking.

John paused a moment at the gate until she came abreast of him, then, shamefacedly, he muttered, 'I'm sorry, madam.'

'That's quite all right.' She was smiling at him. 'He's very happy; and she seems happy too.'

He followed her gaze to where his father was now doing a ring-a-ring-a-roses in the middle of the yard with Bella; and she, too, was singing now, 'Yip! I-addy-I-ay-I-ay.' Then the lady did a strange thing – she put her hand out and touched John's arm, saying softly, 'Don't blame him. And don't be ashamed of him. There are many worse failings than drink, many worse.' And after a moment, during which they stared at each other, she added, 'I'll be walking past . . . Mr Dodd's place; shall I take her back with me? It . . . it might save you a journey.'

'Thank you, if you would.'

He left her standing at the gate and went into the yard. His voice not loud now but firm, he said, 'Father, give over. Stop it. The lady's going to take Bella back home.'

'Oh! Oh, well now, that's kind of her.' He looked towards the gate and lifted his hand towards the woman in what could only be described as a royal gesture. Turning to Bella, whose face was flushed and happy, he said, 'Thank you, my dear. You are a companion after

64

me own heart, and you're a brave little girl not to be afraid of me.'

'Oh, I would never be afraid of you, Mr Thompson. And I don't mind you being drunk 'cos I like you. You're nice.'

'There you are. There you are, son John. What do you think of that? She was aware of me being drunk and she wasn't afraid of me. An' she recognized I was merely drunk, not paralytic or mortalious, just drunk. Oh, La Belle, La Belle Dodd, you are indeed a girl after me own heart. Let me kiss you.'

The next minute Bella found herself held in Mr Thompson's arms and his whisky-laden breath wafting over her, and when he kissed her on both cheeks she put her arms tightly around his neck and kissed him back. He dropped her to the ground again and they both laughed together.

'Come on.' She now felt herself being tugged anything but gently away from the happy drunken man and towards the gate, and as she went she gabbled, 'Oh, give over pulling me like that, John! And why are you vexed? He's a nice father, a lovely father. You're lucky to have . . .'

'Shut up! The lady . . . Mrs Campbell, she's going to take you back home.'

'Oh. Oh' – she turned her head from side to side – 'where is she?'

'Here, my dear.'

As John released her hand the lady took it and, looking over Bella's head, she spoke to John, saying, 'Don't worry,' then added, 'Good-bye.'

'Good-bye, and . . . and thanks.'

'Bye, John. See you the morrer. Will you call for me or will I come up?'

When she received no answer, Mrs Campbell said, 'He's gone. Come along, my dear.'

'He's vexed with his father.'

'Yes, yes, I think he is.'

'I like Mr Thompson; and it's the first time I've seen him drunk. He was nice with it, wasn't he?'

'Yes, yes, he was.'

'Everybody isn't nice when they're drunk.'

'No, I agree with you they're not.'

'How long are you going to stay in your cottage?'

'I'm . . . I'm not quite sure; it all depends.'

'Have you been ill?'

There was a pause before Mrs Campbell answered, 'Yes, I've been ill.'

'Well, you should get better here 'cos the air's good and it makes you eat. I eat a lot, except porridge. Me granda makes it too salty. But it's no use tellin' him; he's stubborn. He likes his own way.'

'Yes, I should imagine so.'

They had traversed about a dozen steps in silence when Bella asked pointedly, 'What colour is your hair, Mrs Campbell?'

'My hair? Why . . . why, it's brown.'

'And your eyes?'

'. . . They are brown too.'

'I've got brown eyes.'

'Yes, yes, you have.'

'John said they're beautiful.'

Mrs Campbell gave a small laugh now before she remarked, 'Did he now?'

'Yes, and he said my skin was like thick cream.'

'Well, well! He takes after his father, because I think Mr Thompson is naturally a very gallant gentleman.'

'Oh no, he doesn't take after his father.'

'No?'

'No, Mr Thompson'll talk and laugh and carry on but John doesn't. He doesn't say very much anytime. You've got to make him talk.'

'But he said you had beautiful eyes and creamy skin.'

'Yes ... yes, he did' – Bella now nodded her head slowly – 'but I had to drag it out of him.'

When Mrs Campbell stopped and began to laugh, Bella listened to her. It was a nice laugh, but when it went on and on and grew louder she asked anxiously, 'Are you all right, Mrs Campbell?'

The laughter died away before Mrs Campbell answered, 'Yes, yes, my dear, I'm all right. I ... I just had a sort of mental picture of you drawing out compliments from your taciturn friend.'

'Tac-i-turn?'

'Well, it means quiet, a bit grumpy.'

'Oh.'

A few minutes later Mrs Campbell exclaimed under her breath, 'Your grandfather is waiting at the gate.'

'He is?' There was a surprised note in Bella's voice; then she added, 'He must like me a bit, mustn't he, if he's on the look out for me?'

Mrs Campbell didn't answer this question for some seconds, and then she said, 'Yes, yes, he must.'

'Hello, Granda.' She had misjudged the distance and was shouting, and when his voice hit her, saying, 'What you yelling your head off for, child?' she answered, 'Oh, I thought you were farther along the road.'

'You're late. Where have you been all this time?'

'Well, you knew John was taking me to the

beach, and . . . and then we were stopped coming back. We had a fight with the Pictons.'

'. . . You had a what?'

'A fight. They set on John, at least one of them did, the one called Gerry, and he knocked him down, I mean, Gerry knocked John down and was knocking steam out of him, but I had a branch in my hand and I went in and lathered him.'

'. . . You went in and what?'

'Well, I've just told you, Granda – I bashed out with it and I cracked him twice. They said he was bleeding but I don't know where. An' I don't much care . . .'

Bella now knew that her grandfather and Mrs Campbell were exchanging glances. She could nearly always tell by the silences what expressions the glances were conveying, but when her grandfather cried, 'Well, that's the last time you go out with him. He's supposed to look after you, not you him,' she cried back at him, 'Wasn't his fault; and that Gerry's a big hulk. I felt it when I hit him.'

'Get yourself inside!'

Bella now turned her face up to Mrs Campbell and said flatly, 'Thank you for bringing me.'

'That's all right, my dear. Perhaps we can have a walk another day.'

'Yes, yes, perhaps we can.'

'Good-day, Mr Dodd.'

Bella knew that her grandfather had half turned away before he answered gruffly, 'Good-day.'

She was taking her hat and coat off in the kitchen when her grandfather said, 'I don't want you to go out walking with that woman.'

'What?'

'You heard.'

68

'But she's nice.'

'Nice is as nice does. I don't like the look of her.'

It was some seconds before Bella said, 'You don't like anybody, do you, Granda?'

'Now don't you be cheeky. I don't want any of your old lip.'

'Well, you don't. You wouldn't like God if the divil was dead.'

As she waited for a response her mouth fell into a gape. Eeh! What had she said? Would he belt her?

When she heard him turn away and make for the door, she scrambled after him and caught at his coat, crying, 'Aw, Granda, I didn't mean it. It was just a sayin' Mrs Golightly used to . . .'

'Be quiet! And don't mention that woman's name to me again. Why do you keep tackin' everything you've ever heard onto her?'

'Because she said it, Granda.'

'Do you know the meaning of lies, child?'

'Yes.'

'Well, do you know that every time you say that she said something you're telling a lie?'

'I am not! I am not so! She does say things like that.'

'Child, she is not real.'

'*She is! She is so, Granda!*'

She knew that he was glaring down at her, and she stared back at him until he said, 'And Gip. Is Gip real?'

Her head drooped now and she turned it to the side.

'Get it into your head, child, that Mrs Golightly is the same as Gip – she's not there, only in your imagination. Even Miss Braithwaite bears this out.'

69

Now her head came up and her tone was defiant again as she said, 'Miss Braithwaite knows nothing about Mrs Golightly, but Miss Talbot does. Miss Talbot knows Mrs Golightly.'

'Then if Miss Talbot knows Mrs Golightly, she's got a lot to answer for. What she should have done instead of encouraging you in your fancies is to skelp your backside. And that's what I'll do if I hear anything more of your Mrs Golightly. Now I'm telling you ... Your tea's on the table; as soon as you've eaten it get yourself up to bed, and not another word out of you.'

When the door banged, she kept her face directed towards it. It couldn't be seven o'clock yet and he was sending her to bed. It would be a long, long time until tomorrow morning.

Automatically she patted her hip now and said sadly, 'Come on, Gip!' then walked towards the table.

4

During the next week a number of things happened that in themselves tended towards her meeting with the new owner of the Manor House. The first was when John came to take her out and her granda sent him off, as he said, with a flea in his ear. A big lad like him, he said, and couldn't take care of a child like her. Not only that, but to get her to fight his battles for him – for it was all over the village that she had split young Picton's head open for him – and she's got a name for herself now as a little wild cat. A chip off the old block, they were saying; and all through that lad not being able to stand on his own two feet.

She had tried to go to John's aid with rapid verbal support, but her granda had actually pushed a brush into her back and thrust her into the kitchen, then closed the door on her.

The next one who called and got a flea in her ear was Mrs Campbell. No, she couldn't take his granddaughter walking. He was delivering some staves and she was going with him.

She had gone with him, sitting up beside him on the front of the cart, having to grab at his coat when they rounded the corners. He had never opened his mouth all the way there or back, and she was so mad at him that she hadn't opened her

71

mouth either, and she determined that she wouldn't speak to him until he spoke to her. But it was a kind of torture to keep her tongue quiet, yet she suffered it until they returned to the house. When she only nibbled at her tea, he said, 'You feeling bad?'

'No,' she said. 'I'm not feeling bad.' And that was all. After she had washed the tea dishes she went upstairs to bed without saying good-night to him. A long time afterwards she heard him standing outside the door before he went into his own room.

The following morning when they were eating their breakfast he said, 'You can help me bundle the staves. I'll show you how.' When she didn't answer him he barked, 'Well, what do you want to do?' And now her reply came quick enough, saying, 'I want to go out with John, or ... Mrs Campbell, or just walk along the road.'

At this, he got up abruptly from the table and went out, and she spent another day kicking her heels.

It was on the Saturday morning that he said to her, 'I've got to go over to the Pictons' with a load, and it will be just as well if they don't see you, so stay put. Go down and play on the path in the wood; but remember what I told you – don't go among the trees.'

After she heard the cart rumbling out of the gate she went to the stable and groped her way along the wall, then over the narrow meadow and to where the guide rope began.

She felt sad. She hadn't talked all week, she hadn't felt anyone's hand or touched anyone, or listened to anyone.

She reached the end of the rope, then made her

way to where the broken wall gave access to the next-door grounds, and as she stood there the smell of the daffodils wafted up to her, and also the other smell that brought her lips into a smile. Narcissi. Oh, she loved the smell of narcissi. It was a distinctive smell, a smell you never forgot. It was coming from quite near. She turned her body about as if she were looking in the direction of the cottage and her grandfather, and then with a defiant toss of her head she swung around and groped her way over the stones of the broken wall.

Oh! Immediately she knew she had trodden on some flower stalks, and she bent down and allowed her fingers to trace the broken stems before picking them up and holding the flowers to her face. Her fingers moving around the serrated edge of the petals, she stood for a moment lost in wonder; then one hand outstretched, she moved forward in what she imagined was a straight line in order that she could return the same way back to the wall. But as she went she realized that she was standing on the flowers, and every now and again she stooped and gathered up the broken ones.

She didn't know how many steps she had taken when she bumped into what she thought was a hedge. When her fingers passed over its prickly fronds, she recognized the tree as a fir tree because it had the same feel as the one that grew by the path on the school drive.

Now she was moving along the hedge, making little exclamations as the fronds whipped her face.

Realizing that she mustn't lose her way, she retraced her footsteps and stopped at the spot opposite where she imagined was the broken wall, and now, sitting down, she began to arrange the flowers she had gathered, the ones with long stalks at the back, those with short stalks at the front.

It was as she sat thus that she heard the foot-steps approaching on the gravel, and the voices, too, and as they came nearer it was as if she could put her hand out and touch the feet, so close were they to her. The voices were those of a man and a woman. The man was saying, 'I'd be pleased to help the minister in any way I can, but at present I can only do so with a donation. I'm going abroad shortly and my agent will be seeing to the renova-tion of the place.'

The lady's voice now said, 'Oh, that is very kind of you. The vicar will be so grateful. We're all look-ing forward to your taking up permanent resi-dence here. It is such a long time since the house was occupied. May I repeat the invitation that you are most welcome to stay at the vicarage until your furniture arrives. I can understand your not wanting to clear your Paris house until the place is ready.'

As the voices faded away Bella thought, That's the gentleman with the voice that's different; but she's got a twang.

She stood up and, her arm extended again, she made for the wall, but immediately on reaching it she realized that her direction had been at fault, for she was in contact with the built-up part. She considered a moment before groping her way to the right, but she still didn't come to the broken part. Now she was moving to the left, and she knew a moment of panic when her feet began to sink into the turf.

Once more she was groping in the opposite

74

direction; but after travelling what was seemingly a long way, she stopped and leaned her back against the wall. She wasn't to know that within another foot of her outstretched hand lay the gap. She was only aware that her granda would be returning shortly and would come looking for her, and if he found she had disobeyed him again, he'd play war. Oh yes, he'd play war all right.

The drive of that house, it . . . it was just beyond the fir hedge. She could crawl underneath the trees and onto it and then walk down to that gate; and once she was on the road she could easily make her way back home – as she now thought of her grandfather's cottage.

Within minutes she was back at the hedge. She gave a sigh of relief when, crawling on her hands and knees, she found wide spaces between the trunks of the firs. Reluctantly now dropping her flowers, because, she told herself, they'd be a dead giveaway if she returned home with them, she crawled through a gap. When she imagined she was clear of the branches she began to stand up, only to be knocked to her knees again. But she didn't cry out, she just laughed inwardly.

Groping forward a few more feet, she knew she was in the open but still on grass, and so, standing up, she stepped tentatively forward again and heaved a deep sigh when her feet touched the gravel drive.

Now standing with her back to the hedge, she knew that the house lay to her left, so the gate must be to her right. Taking the grass verge as a guide, she went slowly ahead. In this way she went some distance and was feeling she must be nearing the gates when she became aware that someone was near her. She stopped and turned her head from side to side and sniffed. She could smell smoke, not tobacco or cigarette but cigar smoke. She knew about cigars because they were what the gentlemen smoked on open days at the school. Cigars had a different smell altogether from cigarettes or tobacco. She didn't care much for the smell of cigars; it made her feel slightly sick. She said aloud now, 'Who's there?'

When the footsteps came towards her she knew that someone had stepped off the opposite verge, and she recognized the voice of the gentleman as he said, 'I should be saying that to you, who's there?'

'I'm . . . I'm lost.'

'Yes, I think you are. You . . . you are the little girl from next door. Mr Dodd's little girl?'

'Yes, sir.'

'Does he know you're out walking by yourself?'

'No, no, sir. He's gone to the Pictons' and . . . and I took a stroll.'

'And you found the gate open and you strolled inside, is that it?'

She waited a moment before she answered him. If she said, 'No, I came over the broken wall and picked some of your flowers,' he might get angry with her, and if he should happen to tell her granda, well, there would be trouble. But it wouldn't be so bad if her granda knew she had walked down the road and come in through the gates.

However, she had no need to answer, for now the gentleman said, 'Come on. I'll put you on your way again.'

She held out her hand and he took it. When they were on the road and he said, 'I'd better see you home,' she answered quickly, 'There's no need, sir. I know me own way up and down the road. I follow the verge.'

'Oh, you're a clever girl.'

'Not very.' Her voice was flat.

He laughed now and said, 'Well, you've got one virtue anyway, you're modest. But if I were you, I wouldn't come near the gates on your walks because . . . well, we're going to have them painted and you don't want to get your clothes all messed up, do you?'

'No, sir. And thank you. But . . . sir!'

'Yes.'

'If you happen to meet me granda, you won't tell him that I was on your drive, will you?'

She felt his breath on her face, and his voice was now a whisper as he said, 'No. No, I won't tell him. That's just a secret between you and me.'

She laughed now and said, 'Thank you, sir.' Then she turned from him and made her way slowly up the road, keeping one foot near the verge.

When Joseph Dodd returned an hour later he found her sitting disconsolately among the wood pile. But when he barked at her, 'All right! Get yourself along the road, but only for an hour, mind,' she sprang up and tripped over some loose poles and fell flat on her face. But she was on her feet almost immediately, crying, 'Oh! Thank you, Granda. Thank you. And I won't stay long. I promise I won't stay long . . .'

After she arrived in the Thompsons' yard she stood for a moment just inside the gate to ascertain the whereabouts of John or his father; but the first voice that came to her was of neither of them – it was the voice of Mrs Campbell. It was coming from the right of her and, it also being

77

slightly muffled, she realized that Mrs Campbell must be in the shed where John said they kept the eggs and vegetables. So she turned in that direction and as she came nearer to the shed Mrs Campbell's voice became clearer. She heard her say, 'What can I do?' And then Mr Thompson's voice answered her, saying, 'Bide your time. See what move he makes next week. It will all depend on his decision.'

'Hello.'

Bella knew that they both started and turned towards her, and it was Mr Thompson who cried, 'Well! Hello there. I thought you had deserted us.'

She moved cautiously towards him because she knew that there should be boxes in the way; but the path in front of her must have been clear because he gave her no warning. When she reached him she put out her hand, which was immediately grasped, and then she said, 'He wouldn't let me out, me granda. It was like being in clink.'

As the roar of laughter greeted this, Harry Thompson cried, 'Where did you hear that?'

'Oh, Mrs Golightly used to say that.'

'Mrs Golightly?'

'Yes.'

The pause and the question mark in Mr Thompson's voice caused her to cry, 'Now don't you say you don't believe in Mrs Golightly, Mr Thompson. Don't be like me granda, 'cos she's real.'

''Course she is, 'course she is, and so is Mrs Campbell here, and you've never said hello to her.'

'Oh! Hello, Mrs Campbell.' She turned sideways, and now her other hand was caught, and the next moment she knew that Mrs Campbell must

78

be sitting on her haunches because of the way her breath was fanning her face. When people bent over you their breath rushed down over your nose, but when they were on a level with you it spread smoothly over your face.

'How are you, Bella?'

'Oh, I'm fine, Mrs Campbell.'

'I've ... I've missed you. I've passed the gate a number of times this week but haven't seen you.'

'Oh, I'd likely be down the wood or in the house. I clean up now and I dust, but he doesn't like things being disturbed ... me granda.'

'Do ... do you like your grandfather?'

'Oh yes, yes, I like him.'

'Would ... would you like to live with him ... for good?'

'Live with me granda for good? Oooh yes! Yes, I would.'

'You don't find him too grumpy?'

'Oh, I don't mind him being grumpy, well, not all the time. I wish he would talk more though, or ... or ...'

'Or what, Bella?'

'Nothin', nothin'.' She shook her head.

'Don't you want to go back to school?'

'Go back to school? Yes, if I could come back at nights. But Miss Braithwaite said I'd likely be sent to a school where you stay all the time, and ... and I wouldn't like that. I ... I like a home, you know, special, like me granda's got.'

She felt Mrs Campbell straightening herself, and when there was silence for a moment, she knew by instinct that again glances were being exchanged, so she put in hastily, 'Me granda's all right. As Mrs Golightly used to say, some people

79

aren't everybody's cup of tea, but it's only because they don't sugar them a bit.'

Again Harry Thompson laughed. And now he rumpled her hair as he said, 'You and your Mrs Golightly! I'd like to meet her some day. She's a store of wisdom that one.'

'Yes, she is, she knows everything. Me dad used to say she knew more than was good for her . . . Where's John?'

'He's along in the greenhouse. Can you find your way?'

'Oh yes. Yes.' She turned about and walked carefully to the door of the shed, and as she passed through it and groped at the wall she heard Mrs Campbell say, 'Dear Mrs Golightly,' and Mr Thompson exclaim, 'What did you say?' and Mrs Campbell reply, 'I said dear Mrs Golightly.'

There was a slight feeling of indignation rising in her when she pushed open the door of the greenhouse and called, 'You there, John?'

'Yes. Hello.'

'Hello.' Carefully she groped her way towards him, and without any preamble she began, 'They don't believe I know a Mrs Golightly, neither your father nor Mrs Campbell. They're . . . they're as bad as me granda.'

'Well, do you?'

'Oh, 'course I know Mrs Golightly!'

'. . . The same as you know Gip?'

She pursed her lips together, swallowed, then turned her head to the side, muttering, 'Gip's different.'

'And Ironsides?'

'I've had a ride on Ironsides.'

80

'I bet.'

'Oh, you!' As she flung round from him his hand caught her shoulder and he said, 'I'm ... I'm sorry. All right, I believe you. You know a Mrs Golightly, and Ironsides, and Gip, so let's leave it at that.'

She now put her hand out and caught at the first thing in front of her, which was a bundle of straw ties, and she began straightening them out with her fingers.

Some minutes passed in silence before, banging the straw down on the rack, she burst out in broken tones, 'Oh, I wish I could see!'

'Aw, there now, Bella, don't cry.'

Impatiently she shrugged off his hand, shouting at him now, 'I'm not cryin', an' I'm not going to cry, because if I started you'd know about it. I can go on for hours, hours and hours ... and days.'

'Don't be silly!' His voice was as harsh as hers now.

'I'm not being silly.'

'What's got into you? ... What's the matter with you, anyway?'

'Nobody believes anything I say.'

'We ... ell' – the word was drawn out – 'you can't blame people really, because you've got a vivid imagination, haven't you? You could write stories the way you think.'

Again there was a silence, broken only when she asked suddenly, 'What's Mrs Campbell really like?'

'Really like, how do you mean?'

'Is she a nice woman?'

'Yes ... I should say she's very nice. And I'm not the only one who ...' He stopped abruptly.

'You were going to say you're not the only one

81

who thinks so? Who else thinks she's nice . . . your father?'

'The things you say! Anyway, why do you ask?'

'I don't know.' She turned, and as she groped towards the bundle of straws again she added, 'I wish I could see her.'

John now bent towards her, looking into her face before saying, 'You've never said that about anybody else. You never said you wanted to see me.'

'Well, I know what you look like.'

'Really?'

'Yes.'

'Well, I can tell you what she looks like. She's got black hair and . . .'

'She hasn't; her hair is brown.'

''Tisn't, it's black.'

'She told me it was brown.'

'You must have made a mistake.'

'I didn't, I didn't. She said that she had brown eyes and brown hair like me.'

'Your trouble is you get things mixed up, like you do people, half real, half fancy.'

'Shut up, you!'

'What's this! What's this!' Harry Thompson's voice now came from the doorway of the greenhouse, and she turned to him quickly and said, 'John says Mrs Campbell's hair is black. It isn't, is it?'

'Well, what I can see of it now,' Harry said quietly, 'it looks black to me, or a very dark brown.'

Bella came slowly down between the racks towards the door and, looking to where she thought Mrs Campbell was standing, she said, 'You told a lie. You said your hair was brown like mine.'

82

There was a long pause before Mrs Campbell replied, 'It was brown like yours, dear, but . . . but I dyed it.'

'Why?'

'Because . . . because I . . . I thought I'd like a change.'

'You're old then?'

'No, no, she isn't old.' Harry Thompson's voice was hearty now. 'She's young, and black or brown her hair's bonny. What do you say, John?'

John swallowed deeply before he muttered, 'Aye, yes, it's nice hair.'

At this his father laughed loudly, saying, 'Well, don't set yourself on fire by paying a compliment, boy. And now, miss, are you satisfied?'

It would be easy to say, 'Yes, Mr Thompson,' but Bella found that she was feeling niggly inside; it was evident to her that both Mr Thompson and John liked Mrs Campbell, and she wanted to like her. Yes, somehow she wanted to like her very much, but there was something stopping her. She didn't know what it was, so what she said was, 'Mrs Golightly says bonny is as bonny does,' and with that she pushed past them and, her hand outstretched, made for the yard gate and the road again. But before she reached it she heard Mr Thompson say, 'No, don't go after her; she'll come round. She's upset about something at the moment. And our Mrs Golightly! I can understand its effect on the old boy. It's enough to drive him mad.'

'Huh!' Bella gave vent to her indignation aloud, then said to no one in particular, 'You wait, just you wait. I'll fetch her, I will. One of these days I'll fetch her up this road and she'll give them the length of her tongue. She will that!'

5

It was the last week of the holidays; there were only four more days to go. The weather had changed again. Last week it had rained most of the time but for the last three days it had been dry but very windy.

She had been with John to the shore again and her grandfather had taken her twice on the cart when he was delivering wood. But what she enjoyed most, she had to admit to herself, was the day that Mrs Campbell had taken her into Newcastle. Mr Thompson had driven them to the station and he was there waiting for them when they came back. But while in Newcastle they had walked by the river, and later had a lovely tea, and Mrs Campbell had bought her, of all things, a toy piano. She could already play six tunes on it with one finger. She could have learned more if her granda hadn't kept on about the racket she was making; but she didn't really mind him going for her about the piano because he had started to talk to her these last few days and ask her questions.

For the past two nights he hadn't sent her to bed but had told her to sit by the side of the fireplace. And tonight even after he had made her cocoa, he hadn't told her to go to bed. He had sat on his chair opposite and smoked his pipe, and he had never once told her to shut up. When she had stopped talking he was so quiet she thought he had fallen asleep, but when she realized he hadn't, she searched her mind for something else that might entertain him, something about grown-ups, and her mind presented her with the very thing. She described to him about the Morgans who had lived in the flat above her and her father, and how when Mrs Morgan ran away, her husband had been so sad that he went up to the top balcony of the flats and threw himself out. It was a long way down and he was all broken up.

Even then her granda hadn't told her to go to bed. She'd had to make the move herself because the heat from the fire had made her sleepy. And now here she was in bed and getting wider and wider awake. Things always went contrary.

She didn't know at what time she fell asleep, nor at what period the nightmare started, but it began with Mr Morgan's face looking at her through the doorway. The next time she saw Mr Morgan he was climbing the stairs and his head was hanging right down on his chest. Then again he was looking at her through the doorway, but now his head was bobbing towards her. And then she imagined herself sitting up in bed looking at Mr Morgan as he sat at the foot, waving his hand to her. All of a sudden she saw him lean back and tumble downwards. When he passed their iron balcony she jumped after him and tried to catch him. But she stopped on the last balcony because when he hit the ground his body broke into hundreds of pieces and the blood squirted from

85

him and right up into her eyes and she couldn't see anything.

It was at this point she screamed, scream upon scream.

'Stop it. For God's sake, stop it!'

She knew it was her granda and that he was shaking her by the shoulders, but she couldn't stop screaming because she could smell the blood on her face.

When he let go of her she dropped back on the pillow, and then she felt for a moment that she had jumped from the iron balcony, so far did she leap up in the bed when the cold wet flannel came smack across her face.

'Oh, Granda! Granda! You shouldn't, you shouldn't. I . . . I was just dreamin'.'

'Just dreamin'! Anyone would think you were being murdered, child. Here, dry your face.' He thrust a towel at her, and after rubbing it around her face she gasped, 'It was Mr Morgan, the man who threw himself out of the window. I . . . I thought . . .'

'Never mind what you thought! Stop thinking about Mr Morgan and lie down and get yourself to sleep. Three o'clock in the morning!'

'I'm . . . I'm sorry, Granda.'

There was a pause before he said, 'It was only a dream. Remember that it was only a dream.'

'Yes, Granda.'

As she heard his footsteps going towards the door she said in a small voice, 'Granda! . . . Could I come and sleep with you?'

'What!'

'Just . . . just for the night.'

'Don't talk nonsense, child. Get yourself to sleep.'

As the door banged, the fear swept over her again, but as quickly as the door had closed it was opened and her grandfather's voice came to her, saying now, 'I'll leave your door open, and mine, so you're all right, do you hear? Now get to sleep.'

'Yes, yes, Granda.'

Oh, that was better. It was like sleeping in the same room when their doors were open. She drew in a long breath, turned on her side, and within a few moments she was fast asleep again.

It was what you called a slack morning. John wasn't coming for her until after dinner, and Mrs Campbell had gone into Fellburn yesterday and hadn't come back yet. Her grandfather was at the sawing block. There was nothing to do really, so she decided to take a walk through the wood. Calling Gip to her, she said, 'Steady now. And don't run away like you did yesterday.' And in this fashion she talked to him until she came up to the broken wall; and there she stopped and sniffed. The daffodils were finished but the narcissi she smelled were still going strong. She turned and faced the way she had come; then looking down at Gip, she said, 'He wouldn't know, and I won't pick any, at least unless I trample on them.' She turned about again and, on her hands and knees, scrambled over the broken masonry and into the grassy and flower-strewn belt. But once clear of the stones she stopped. She had lost her way last time, hadn't she? Well, she wouldn't be so silly this time; she'd leave herself a guide. She would pick the smallest stones and space them at intervals towards the fir trees, then she could move a little way to each side of them and not get lost.

It took her quite some time to sort out the smallest stones, the ones she was able to lift and carry, and to place them so many steps apart in a more or less straight line until she came to the boundary of firs.

After placing the last stone near the root of a fir tree, she was on the point of moving in the direction of where the scent of the narcissi was strongest when she stopped and, her head cocked to one side, she listened. Something was moving in the undergrowth almost at her feet. Was it an animal? a fierce animal? She stiffened and waited for it to approach; but it didn't come towards her yet continued to rustle. Perhaps it was a rabbit burrowing. No, a rabbit would have run away, and a dog or a cat would have come out. But it couldn't be a very big animal because the branches of the fir tree spread down and reached just below her waist; if she should want to pass under them she would have to crawl.

The rustling stopped, but after some seconds when it began again she dropped down onto her knees and moved forward under the outspread branches until her groping hands touched the trunk; and then, moving from it, they touched something else that made her start back. What she had touched was a coat sleeve and there was an arm inside it.

She waited to be grabbed, but when no hand touched her she said, 'Who's there?' Her voice was a throaty whisper, and the answer seemed to come in the form of a vigorous rustle among the dry leaves.

Again she put her hand out, and now she almost cried out aloud as her fingers touched skin, prickly skin, a chin, like her dad's used to be when he hadn't shaved. As she was withdrawing her hand her fingers came in contact with something else, material; but it was across the face. After a moment's hesitation her fingers began exploring, and her eyes opened wide as she realized it was a piece of cloth, and it was tight across a mouth. Now her hand moved rapidly over a nose, a big nose, and onto another piece of cloth, across the eyes this time.

When slowly she pulled the cloth upwards the body wriggled vigorously and she knew that the eyes were staring up into hers. She whispered haltingly, 'I ... I can't see you, I'm ... I'm blind,' and again there was a violent movement of the body.

It seemed to her in this moment that she heard Mrs Golightly's voice yelling at her, 'Well, you're not deaf! Unloosen that thing around his mouth and he'll speak to you.'

Her hands now rapidly found their way to the double knot at the back of the head, and when she pulled the cloth away from the face she heard a great gasp. And now the voice was whispering at her, a man's voice, 'Can you unloosen my hands, little girl? Can you hear me?'

'Yes, yes, I can hear you.'

'Unloosen my hands.'

She was about to bend further down to where she thought the man's hands were when he said, 'Ssh!' and she became still, for she, too, heard the sound of footsteps coming across the gravel. Then he was whispering at her, 'Go and get help. Go and tell your parents, tell them they have taken me ...' He didn't finish but cried at her under his breath, 'Go! Go!' She scrambled

89

backwards under the branches and, still on her hands and knees and aiming to go softly, she guided herself by the stones until she reached the broken wall. Once there, she crouched down behind it, instinct telling her to remain still. As she did so she heard muttered exclamations from beyond the fir trees, then crashing movements, and someone coming into the clearing.

Her heart seemed to be beating loudly in her ears as the footsteps came towards the wall, then stopped just a short distance away, and she knew that whoever was there was looking up the grass path through the wood. Then in answer to a hissing hail, she heard the footsteps going back towards the hedge, and a scathing voice mutter, 'Tie a knot! You couldn't even pass for the Brownies. Go round to the stable and see if the coast's clear now. Cor, another minute an' we'd have bumped right into them, and the lid would have been blown off all right then.'

This scathing remark and order was answered by an oath that made her bite on her lip; then she heard the footsteps on the gravel again.

She remained crouched against the wall, telling herself that who knew but there might still be somebody watching her.

It seemed a long, long time before she allowed herself to move. She made a quick dash, managed to grasp the rope, then ran as hard as her legs would carry her up through the wood. But not until she reached the yard did she call out, 'Granda! Granda!'

'What is it? Stop your pelting, you'll be on your face in a minute.'

'Granda! Granda!' She flung herself against his legs and, her two hands now grabbing at his waistcoat, she gabbled, 'A man. There's a man. He was all tied up under the trees, the fir trees near the drive.'

'What on earth are you talking about, child?'

'Granda, listen!' She tugged at his waistcoat again. 'His hands and legs are tied. I . . . I took the bandage off his eyes and the one around his mouth, and he told me to get help.'

She felt her hands smacked away from the waistcoat; and now her granda was bawling at her. 'Now look here, miss! We had enough of nightmares in the night; it's broad daylight, so stop your fancyising, do you hear me, child, before you drive me distracted.'

She stood away from him, one hand held tightly under an armpit. The slap had hurt her, and now she gulped before she said slowly, 'Granda! Please listen, Granda. I'm not fancyising. I'm not, honest. God's honour, I'm not. I went over the wall. I know I shouldn't because you told me I shouldn't, but it was the smell of the narcissi, and I was bending down and there he was underneath the branches, and he was all tied up. I . . . I thought it was an animal.'

'Child!' The word held deep reproach; and now she bowed her head and there were tears in her voice as she said, 'Oh, Granda, Granda! I'm not puttin' it on, I'm not tellin' the tale. When I took the bandage off his eyes I told him I couldn't see him, and . . . and then he wriggled and I took the one from his mouth and he asked me to loosen his hands. And then we heard them coming, the men, and he said, "Go and get help. Go and tell your parents." '

She knew now that her grandfather was bending forward, peering at her. Then she felt

91

him straighten up, and when he walked away from her she could, in her mind's eye, see him looking down through the wood. Now he was back bending down to her again and his voice was deep and solemn as he said, 'You're not having me on, child? Swear you're not having me on.'

'I swear, Granda.' She crossed her heart with her fingers.

'Come on.' He was striding away; and she was hanging on to his belt now for he hadn't bothered to put his coat on.

When they reached the broken wall she whispered to him, 'I . . . I put some stones to guide me; they're not big ones but you'll be able to see them.'

When she felt him cautiously crossing over the broken wall, she followed him. When he stopped for a moment before going on again, she knew he had seen the stones.

Now she was by his side, tugging at his sleeve to make him kneel down; then she crawled forward and her hands groped here and there on the grass but touched nothing but small, broken twigs and dead leaves.

When she felt herself pulled back she stood up and whispered, 'He's gone! They've taken him.'

She shivered as she heard the long, hissing breath escaping through her granda's lips; then simultaneously they both heard the sound of voices and movements on the gravel, and he placed his hand on her shoulder in a tight grip, which warned her to remain still and to be silent.

The sound she heard now she knew to be that made by horses' hooves, but above them there came the voices of people talking. There seemed to be a number of people and their voices were pleasant. One was a lady's voice and she was saying, 'Well, we won't give you any peace, Mr Aimsford, until you promise to join us.' Then came another voice that she decided Mrs Golightly would term high falutin' because it seemed to come out of the top of the speaker's head as he said, 'Yes, yes, Aimsford; as my wife says, we won't give you any peace, and we can loan you a mount until you get settled.' Then came the gentleman's voice that she recognized, and his voice sounded gay and airy as he replied, 'Rest assured that on my return I shall take you at your word, and then you won't be able to get rid of me.' Laughter followed this remark, and then the voices and the sound of the horses' hooves faded into the distance.

Just as she was about to speak she felt herself almost lifted bodily from the ground, for her granda was gripping the collar of her coat. Her feet were straining to touch the ground as he hauled her back over the stones and along the wood path. He didn't speak until they reached the yard, but there, letting go of her collar, he swung her around to face him and his voice was a deep growl as he said, 'A man trussed up and taken into that house! And I suppose under the very nose of Lord and Lady Committy, eh?'

She was trembling from head to foot and her voice was a stammer now as she said, 'Gra ... Granda, there ... there was.'

'Shut up! Shut up this minute! Don't let me hear another word out of you. I saw them with my own eyes, Mr Aimsford and his lordship and her going down the drive, leading their horses. They must have been in that house or yard for some time. Those two don't make short visits, not when they mean to latch on to anyone with money. Poor as church mice they might be, but never so poor as not to have enough money for their horses. Horse mad they are. But they're not the only ones that are mad. No . . . no, child!'

She knew now that his face was quite close to hers as he repeated, 'Child, I'm warning you. There'll come a day when your imagination will be the ruin of you. Do you hear me?'

She made no answer; her throat was tight. She wanted to cry but she knew she mustn't because he'd have no pity for her if she started to cry now, and who would see to her?

'Now get yourself into the house there and don't move till that boy comes and fetches you. Do you hear me? And be back here by three. Do you hear me? No later. When I come back from the trip I expect you in.'

She didn't answer but turned and, putting her hands out, groped at the air as she walked forward, only to find herself grabbed again by the neck and turned around in the direction of the back door; and his hold on her wasn't released until he had pushed her into the scullery and banged the door behind her.

She sat on the chair in the kitchen rocking herself backwards and forwards, her two hands gripping the arms. That poor man – what would they do to him? There had been a man there, hadn't there? She had untied the bandage from around his mouth and from over his eyes? She stopped her rocking and asked a question of the empty room. 'I did feel him, didn't I? I wasn't dreaming, was I?'

Then she answered herself, 'No, you weren't

94

dreaming. There was a man there all tied up.'

She wished John were here; she wished she could go to him straightaway. But would he believe her? In a way he was very like her granda.

But she'd have to make somebody believe her. Mrs Campbell. Yes, Mrs Campbell would believe her. But Mrs Campbell was away in Fellburn. Mr Thompson. Yes, Mr Thompson would likely believe her. If John didn't believe her she would go straight to his father.

But they could have killed that poor man by then. By! If they had, and he was found, her granda would have a very red face. By! He would that. And it would bring him down a peg, lots of pegs, and when he said to her he was sorry she would say, 'It's too late to be sorry.' That's what Mrs Golightly said. A time came, she said, when it was too late for people to say they were sorry. She had said that the day she had come in and found her dad crying; and she had said he only managed to say he was sorry when he was drunk and that it would be a different kettle of fish if he ever said he was sorry when he was sober.

It seemed to be easier for people to say they were sorry when they'd had a drop.

On this conclusion she decided that even if they did find the man dead, her granda wasn't very likely to take the blame to himself, for he never took a drop.

They had walked up the road towards the small holding, arguing all the time, and now at the gate John threatened her: 'Look! If you don't stop talking such nonsense, I'm going to take you straight back to your granda and tell him why.'

'I won't go with you.'

95

'We'll see about that.'

'You're just like him, you believe nothing.'

'I can't believe you. You've told me that your granda went back with you and there was nobody there, and then you heard Lord and Lady Committy on the drive with Mr Aimsford. Now use your sense if you've got any. During the time you left that man, or the one you imagined was there, until you got back to the spot with your granda must have only been a matter of minutes, ten at the most, and by the sound of it the visitors must have been there some time. People like them don't come and pay a visit and say "How do you do?" and walk out again, so how do you think they managed to get a trussed-up man into the house, past those big windows?'

'They . . . they needn't have taken him into the house. There's bound to be stables and things. They could have put him in there.'

'I know that place, Bella.' Now his voice held a long-suffering, patient note. 'It's been empty on and off for years. Nobody seems to stay. And I've played round there and in the stables. But the stables lie at yon side of the house. There's a big courtyard with outhouses on three sides of it, but there are no buildings on this side where you were standing. It's just woodland. Your granda's wood was once part of the property; it was one of the bits that was sold off years ago. It used to be a big estate at one time; now there's only the house and about twelve acres left. And the out-houses are all at yon side as I said, so I ask you, how would those fellows that you thought you heard . . .?'

'*I did hear them!* And I heard them swearin'.'

'All right, all right, you heard them. Well, how

do you think they got a trussed-up body past those windows that go practically down to ground level? Both the drawing and dining room windows are facing the drive. I tell you I know that house. I've explored it from the attic that used to be the nursery right down to the cellar, the coal cellar. There are no real cellars. So now what do you want to do? Are you going to shut up about it or are you going back home?'

She was feeling sick; there was an upheaval in her chest. She turned about and retched. Holding her head and his voice full of concern, John said, 'Oh, Bella, why do you get so upset? Why do you think such things? Get it up! That's it.' But she was unable to make any retort.

When she had finished vomiting up the dinner her grandfather had insisted she eat, she lifted her head and muttered, 'A drink of water.'

'Come along.' His voice and attitude were now full of concern, and when a few minutes later she was sitting in the kitchen sipping a glass of water, he got down on his haunches before her and, his voice unusually soft, he said, 'I ... I want to believe you, Bella, but everything is against it. You see, you're always imagining things, aren't you? Now own up. There's the dog, and the horse, and Mrs Golightly. . .'

'Mrs Golightly is real, and ... and the horse too.'

'And Gip?'

Her head drooped. 'No, no,' she said. 'I made Gip up a long time ago 'cos I hadn't anyone to talk to, and now he's sort of real to me. I can nearly see him. But ... but' – and now she put her hand out and groped towards him – 'Mrs Golightly is real, John. And the horse is too. And ... and the man who was trussed up ... Don't sigh like that, John, I'm telling you the truth ... Have you – ?' She turned her head now from side to side, then said rapidly, 'Have you got a Bible?'

'A Bible?'

She knew his face was screwed up.

'Well, if anybody swears on a Bible and it isn't the truth, then they can expect to go to hell for ever and ever. Have you got a Bible?'

She knew he was standing up now, and he said quietly, 'Yes, yes, we have a Bible.'

'Can you get it?'

She waited patiently until he returned to her and placed the book in her hand. Handing him the glass, she placed one hand on top of the book and, closing her eyes, said solemnly, 'Our Father who art in Heaven, hallowed be Thy name. You know I speak the truth when I say I felt a man trussed up under the fir tree and that when I took the bandage from his mouth and eyes he asked me to go for help. 'Tell your parents,' he said. And then the other men came. You know they did, Lord, don't you? And you know I'm speaking the God's truth ... Amen.'

Slowly now she handed the Bible back to John. He took it without a word, but it was some minutes before he moved from her side and placed it on the table. Then coming to her again, he said quietly, 'What time was this when ... when you went down to the wood the first time?'

She had pulled herself off the chair and was standing close to him, her face turned up towards his as she said, 'It was a good while after breakfast. You see, I'd had a nightmare and woke up yelling and disturbed me granda and ... and he wasn't in a good temper, so I didn't go near him

98

at the sawing block. I felt I'd better keep out of his way for a while. I walked about the yard for a bit and then went to the gate and . . .'

'What time do you usually have your breakfast?'

'Oh, eight o'clock, because he always puts the wireless on then. That's the only time he lets it be on, to get the news and the time.'

'How long did you play round the yard, do you think?'

'Oh, about half an hour or more. But before that I washed up and tidied the kitchen and I made my bed and dusted my room. I mustn't have gone outside till quite a long time after nine o'clock . . . What time is it now?'

'Just turned three.'

'He could be dead; they could have killed him.'

'Well, who could they be?' he asked her now. 'I don't know if Mr Aimsford has more than one man working for him. I saw a man on the drive as I was passing, but it was in the distance and I didn't recognize him. And with regard to this . . . this man being dead, if they were going to kill him they would have done it before now, I should imagine, not trussed him up and brought him here . . . And there's another thing.'

'What?'

'Well, there's no news in the paper about anybody being kidnapped or anything like that. You sometimes hear of people being kidnapped and held to ransom for money, but it's always in the papers. I went to the village and got this morning's paper for Father and there were no headlines to that effect. What I should do now is to take you down to the village to see Constable Samson, but what he would do immediately would be to come back and see your granda to confirm what you'd said, and then ... well, we know what would happen after that, don't we?'

'Yes.' Her voice was small. 'So ... so what are you going to do?'

She knew he had turned from her and was thinking. When he turned to her again, he said, 'I know how to get into the grounds from yon side. I've come up into the stable yard many a time that way. I could have a look into the outhouse, because if the owner, Mr Aimsford, expects visitors like Lord and Lady Committy, then they would never have taken the man into the house. But still –'He paused and she knew he was pondering on something, so she said, 'What is it?'

'Well, if it's not in the papers about a man being missing, who can he be? Perhaps he's of no importance except ... well, he could be one of their own men, somebody that had done them down in some way.'

'Would that stop you letting him loose?'

Again he paused before answering, and then he said, 'No, no, I suppose not.' And he added, 'I wish Father was home.'

'Has he gone to the village?'

His bark made her start when he cried, 'No, he hasn't! He hasn't been to the village for days.'

'Oh. Oh, I wasn't meaning anything. I didn't mean the pub, I just meant had he ... had he taken some eggs and vegetables in, or something like that? You needn't go down me throat.'

'I'm ... I'm sorry.'

'Anyway, I don't see why you get so het up about your da takin' a drop, 'cos he's a nice man.'

'He'd be a nicer if he kept sober.'

'Eeh! You are like me granda in some ways,

100

John. But don't let us fight, not until you see where that man is.'

She heard him drawing in a long breath and letting it out before saying, 'Well, come on. If we intend to push our noses into somebody else's affairs, we'd better do it before I start doubting again . . .'

Ten minutes later they passed the gates of the drive that led up to the old manor house, but it wasn't until they were well past that John said under his breath, 'There's nobody about as far as I can see.'

They had gone some distance farther along the road when he said, 'Come on, you've got to jump a ditch here and go along by the boundary fence, or what they call a fence, for there's hardly any of it left standing. Farmer Pollock's cattle have trampled it down in parts.'

After she had jumped the ditch she held on to him tightly until he stopped walking when, putting his lips close to her ear, he said, 'Now don't say anything, not a word, unless I speak to you. Do you hear?'

'Yes.'

'And if I hear anything and want to bring you to a quick stop, I'll squeeze your hand. But then, with your ears you'll likely hear sounds before I do, so if you want to draw my attention, press my hand twice, like this.' He demonstrated.

'All right.' Her whisper held a tremor, but it was more of apprehension than excitement.

Now he was leading her through a winding path and every now and again the brambles that he parted sprang back and hit her, and more than once she felt like shouting out. Then they were in the clear again, and his lips were near her ear, saying, 'I can see the entrance to the courtyard. I think you'd better stay here until I go and have a look.'

'No, no! Please take me with you. I'll be more frightened here.'

'But if anybody sees me I've got to run for it.'

'I can run too.'

'You won't be able to run through the thicket and I might have to make a dash for it. Now look, I'll explain where you are. You're standing with your back to a young birch tree, and right opposite to you is the arch leading into the courtyard. Now don't move from there until I get back.'

'Oh, John!'

'Never mind "oh, John." Now do what I tell you.'

'Be careful.'

'Don't worry, I'll be careful. I don't want to be trussed up too.'

She knew he was smiling at her but she didn't smile back. Then she heard his footsteps going softly over the grass, and when she could hear them no longer she knew he had gone through the arch.

From the moment she realized she was alone, she told herself to count the seconds and that's how she'd know how long he had been away.

She had just finished counting sixty for the fifth time when she heard a yell and a voice cry, 'Leave me a -- !' The rest was smothered in a scuffling of feet on the stone yard. When this sound continued and was intermingled with grunts and broken words, she left the tree and rushed towards the opening, calling, 'John! John!' As she did so a voice cried, 'My God! There's another of 'em.' She turned about and made to scramble back towards the tree, but found herself plunging into the undergrowth.

At the same time as a bramble branch caught her fully across her face, two hands gripped her shoulders and heaved her backwards. When she yelled, a hand was placed tightly across her mouth, and she felt she was going to choke. Now she used her arms and her legs, and she clawed and kicked at the man who was holding her to such purpose that when he had managed to pin her arms, he called throatily between curses to someone to come and hold her legs.

Now she felt herself being lifted up bodily; hands were gripping her ankles, another hand was encompassing her wrists, while yet another still pressed tightly against her mouth.

She was being carried through the yard, and the throaty voice of the man who had his hand across her mouth called to someone, 'Where, boss?' A voice from the distance came in what was almost an undertone, saying, 'The room cellar.'

A few minutes later she felt herself being carried through an enclosed place; then she knew they were taking her, head first, down the steps. At the bottom, when she became horizontal again, a voice said, 'Let her go.'

'What if she screams?'

'She could scream her head off down here and nobody would hear her, not at this end.'

When she hit the ground none too gently she lay still, panting, making no movement.

Presently, the first voice said, 'What about the lad? Have you knocked him out completely?'

'He'll survive . . . Bloody kids! Last thing one would expect to happen. The whole bloody police force, aye, but not kids. And one of them as blind as a bat!'

'Shut your mouth! You talk too much.'

'Talk too much? If I hadn't caught him we might have been talkin' to a bleeding judge shortly. Nothin's gone right with this lot, nothin'.'

'Will you shut up! If the boss hears you, nothin'll go right for you. You know that, don't you? You're a damn fool. Go on, get up!'

The voices faded away. There was the sound in the distance of a door clanging closed, then quiet blackness and deep silence all around her. She was used to the blackness but the silence was heavy and frightening. Her voice was a mere whimper as she said tentatively, 'John.' Then again, 'John!'

When there was no answer, she turned onto her hands and knees and began to grope around her. One thing was evident straightaway – the stone floor was very dusty and it was cold.

Her voice now was louder and threaded with panic as she called, 'John! John! Are you there? John! John! Where are you?' She had come up against an obstruction, not one but many. Her fingers, moving swiftly, made them out to be boxes, small boxes, big boxes, different shaped boxes. She turned and rested her back against one and began to whimper, 'Oh, John! Oh, Granda! Oh, dear me! Oh, dear me!'

It was just as real panic was about to rise in her that she heard the slight rustle. It was to the right of her and she turned her head eagerly in its direction. When it came again and was followed by a moan, she scrambled forward, crying loudly, 'John! John!'

'Oh, my goodness!'

As her hands passed over his face, then gripped

104

his shoulders, he pushed her aside and, pulling himself up, said again, 'Oh, my goodness!' and now added, 'Oh, my head!'

'Are you all right?'

'No.' The word was half a groan. 'No, I'm not all right. It's my head.'

When her fingers moved over his head he winced and said, 'Oh! Careful.'

'There's a big bump on it. They must have hit you with something hard.'

'I'll say they did. Is it bleeding?'

Her fingers went tentatively through his hair and she said, 'It isn't wet.'

'It feels as if it's been split in two . . . Where are we, anyway? It's . . . it's dark . . . black.'

When she detected a slight note of panic in his voice she said, 'It's all right. I . . . I can find me way around in the dark, so stay still and I'll go and . . .'

'Don't be silly!' He thrust her aside and stood up, saying, 'There must be a window, there must be light of some kind.'

She heard him moving forward, only to exclaim loudly as he stumbled over the boxes, and she cried at him, 'I told you, I told you. You won't be able to find your way if it's dark. Put your hands out when you're walking.'

'I had them out.'

'Ssh! Listen!' she said.

'What is it?'

'There's . . . there's somebody coming. I heard a door opening in the distance.'

He cocked his head from one side to the other but heard nothing for a moment; in fact, he heard no noise whatsoever until the sound of a key grating in a lock came to him, and then the

105

further sound of a door opening, a door that he guessed was little used if the grating of the hinges was anything to go by. Then he was gazing upwards to the top of a long flight of stone steps and to the figure of a man who appeared faceless in the light of the candle he was holding aloft.

As Bella's hand touched his, he pulled her to his side and stood stiff, yet trembling, as he watched the man descend the steps; and on his approach he saw the reason for his featureless face – he had a stocking pulled over his head. It also muffled his voice as he said, 'Interfering young fool! You've got yourself into a mess now, haven't you?'

'Not as much a mess as you'll be in when they catch you.'

'Now, none of your old lip. You're in trouble as it is so don't worsen it by gettin' me back up.'

'You can't keep us here.'

'Can't we? Well, that remains to be seen.'

'They'll be searching for us.'

'Aye, likely they will, lad, but who'd expect to find you in Mr Aimsford's house, at least under it, well under it? I don't suppose there's half a dozen people know of this particular cellar 'cos there's no way out except through that door up there. But that only leads into a gap, and beyond that is a wall and that wall's all of two feet thick. Anyroad, I'm leaving you these candles.' He now put his hand in the pocket of his reefer coat and brought out three candles, adding, 'Be sparin' with 'em 'cos these are all you'll get.'

The man turned sideways and was placing the candles on one of the many boxes when he was startled into a rain of curses as Bella's hands found his arm and, hanging on to it, she kicked at his shins, shouting, 'Get him, John! Get him, John!'

The next moment it was she who yelled as she was lifted up by the hair and flung aside. Then the man was backing towards the stairs, glaring at John as he yelled, 'Don't you try anything, youngster. This is what I get for bein' decent. If I'd done what they said I'd have left you in the dark. As for that little vixen, for two pins I'd . . .' He didn't finish the sentence but turned abruptly and ran up the stairs.

As the light disappeared and the door banged, John groped his way towards the box where the man had left the candles and matches. Having lit a candle, he held it above his head and looked about him. Then looking at Bella, he said, 'Are you all right?'

'Yes.' And now she added in a small voice that was almost a whimper, 'I'm . . . I'm sorry, John. I'm sorry I've got you into this trouble.'

'No need to be sorry; you were right. It's that grandfather of yours who should be sorry.'

'Then . . . then you saw the man?'

'Yes. Yes, I caught a glimpse of him. I think they were just about to move him. He was at the end of the coach house, trussed up like a chicken.'

'They're bad men.'

'You're telling me.'

'Where are we? What is it like?'

After a moment John said, 'It's a cellar of some sort and it must be pretty deep because there are quite a number of steps up to that door. And –' He paused and, walking from her to the far wall, he said, 'This seems to be the only flat bit that we're on now; the floor seems to slope upwards but for most of the way it's piled up to the roof with boxes, all kinds of boxes, like packing cases.' He now turned one of the boxes over and added, 'This one's got straw inside. Looks as if they've been used for packing glass or china.'

'John.'

'Yes, what is it?'

'Why don't we go up the stairs and listen at that door?'

'What good will that do? You heard him, he said there was a wall behind, beyond.'

'Well, I might be able to hear something.'

'You?'

'Yes. I told you I can hear things that other people can't. It's because ... well, I'm ... I'm kind of listenin' all the time.' She held out her hand and whispered, 'Take me up.'

Without further ado, he took hold of her hand and led her to the foot of the stone stairs, saying, 'Hold tight, they're steep and there's no railing on that side, and if you fall over you could break your neck.'

'Twenty-three.'

'What?'

'There's twenty-three steps.' She was whispering now. Then when her hand moved over the door in front of her she said, 'Where's the keyhole?'

When he directed her to the keyhole, she put her ear to it while he held the candle above her head and looked down on her.

The silence was heavy about them. He could hear nothing, yet after a few seconds, when her grip on his hand tightened, he knew that she could hear something, so he bent his head down to hers and put his ear to the wood. But still no sound came to him except that of her quick breathing.

She must have kept her position at the keyhole for all of three to four minutes before she straightened up. Then she whispered, 'They've gone.'

'Who?'

'Them and the gentleman.' She was tugging at his hand now, indicating that they should go down the steps, and when they reached the floor of the cellar again he demanded sharply, 'Well, out with it! What did you hear?'

For a moment she didn't reply; then her words came slow as if she herself couldn't believe what she was saying. 'It was the gentleman talking.'

'The gentleman?'

'Yes, the one who owns the house.'

'Don't be silly . . . Yet wait! How could all this go on without him knowing? But how did you know it was him?'

'By his voice, of course. He's got a different voice, a gentleman's voice.'

'Lots of men speak like him.'

'No, not like him; his voice is different. I know voices. I tell people by their voices and he was talking to the man who had just been down here and another man, and he hadn't closed the door – the other door, or whatever it is.'

'Could you hear what they were saying?'

'Not much, except when the gentleman shouted.'

'What did he say?'

'He swore, and then he said they were idiots. Then he said something like, if they couldn't get him across tonight it would mean them hanging on for another day, and the fish man said . . .'

109

'The fish man! What are you talking about?'

'The man who was down here. He ... he smelled of fish. Couldn't you smell it?'

'No.'

'Well, anyway, it was him who said it was impossible to get him across tonight 'cos the boat wasn't due until tomorrow. Then the gentleman swore again and said, how could they get him away tomorrow, for by then the roads would be swamped with people looking for ... them two ... He was meaning us ... Oh, they will look for us, won't they, John?'

The effect on him of the tremor in her voice was now making it difficult for him to keep his own voice steady as he replied, 'Yes, of course they will. Your ... your grandfather will be scouring the roads already.'

'And ... and your da too.'

'Yes, yes, Dad'll be worried.' He didn't voice the thought and add, 'If he comes back sober.'

'Fish.'

'What! What did you say?'

'Fish, the man smelled of fish.'

'Well, what can you make of that?'

'He ... must be a fisherman.'

'A fisherman!' He paused a moment; then gripping her arm, he shook it, saying excitedly, 'Yes, yes, you're right, he is a fisherman, and I know who he is. Somehow I thought I recognized him, the size of him, and then something about his voice although it was muffled. He's Dick Riley from the village. He does odd jobs about the countryside, but mostly he helps Mr Benbow, Andrew Benbow. He's got a boat. He was brought up for lobster poaching last year. You know something?' He was bending over her now.

110

'I bet you what you like they intend to take that man somewhere by sea.' He straightened up, bit on his lip, then finished, 'I wonder who he is. He must be someone important and they're holding him for ransom.'

'Then they won't kill him?'

He now made himself say, 'No, no, they won't kill him,' all the while thinking, You never know what they'll do to him, and to us, if they get desperate enough.

As if Bella had picked up his thoughts she said softly, 'Do you think they'll kill us, John?'

'No, don't be silly.'

'I'm cold.'

'Here, take my coat.'

'No, no.' She put out her hands to prevent him taking off his coat, saying, 'You'll be cold then . . . but . . . but didn't you say there was straw and shavings in those boxes?'

'Yes. Yes, that's an idea. But look out where you're going! Don't knock the candle out of my hand. I'd better stick it down and then when we're settled I'll put it out, 'cos he's only left the three and I don't know how long they'll have to last.'

After dripping some grease onto the floor near the wall he stuck the candle on it, then said, 'Now you stay where you are, because these boxes are all piled up higgledy-piggledy and they'll come tumbling down about our ears if we're not careful. I'll hand you the straw and you can lay it out on the floor, like a bed, you know.'

'Yes, yes.'

It took him quite some time to get enough straw out of the boxes to make a rough pallet bed, and when it was finished they sat down side by side.

Neither of them spoke for some minutes, and

111

when in a small voice she said, 'Will you hold my hand, John?' he took it between his own and rubbed the cold fingers for a moment as he said with more confidence than he felt, 'Don't be afraid. It's all right. They can't keep us here for long. They wouldn't dare.'

Again they were quiet, until she murmured something so softly that he was unable to hear, and so, bending towards her, he said, 'What did you say?'

'I . . . I want to go to the lavatory . . .'

He swallowed, clicked his tongue, blinked, then said abruptly, 'Come on.'

He led her now towards the wall, saying, 'There's a passage up here where I've cleared the boxes. Keep against the wall or you'll have them on top of you.' He just stopped himself from pushing her forward, and when she said, 'You needn't wait,' he turned abruptly away and returned to where the candle was set. He took it from the floor and went back to their makeshift bed, and having sat down, he snuffed it out.

'John!' Bella's voice came from the corner of the room. "Talk to me and I'll know where you are.'

'Over here, this way.'

As she flopped down beside him, she said, 'What's that burning smell?'

'I put the candle out.'

'Are you hungry?'

'More thirsty than hungry.'

'Do you think they'll give us anything to eat?'

'That remains to be seen.'

They sat in silence for quite a while until John, in an unusually gentle tone, said, 'Bella.'

'Yes, John?'

'I . . . I never realized before what it . . . well, don't mind me saying this, but what it meant to be in black darkness.'

When she groped for his hand he held hers tightly, and when she said, 'Don't be frightened, you get used to it,' he didn't put on a brave act and say, 'Frightened! I'm not frightened.' What he did say was, 'I . . . I don't think I'd ever get used to it, Bella. I . . . I don't know how you can keep so bright and cheerful.'

'Oh, that's nothing. As Mrs Golightly used to say, it's me nature. If I'd been born without hands and feet, she said, I'd have been the same. She said I throw light on diversity, or something like that.'

'Oh, Mrs Golightly. She must have been a kind of sage, your Mrs Golightly.'

'Sage? Sage is what you put in stuffin'.'

He gave a shaky laugh as he replied, 'In this case it means wise. She always seemed to be coming out with wisecracks.'

'She said most of them when she was tight.'

Bella now knew that he had turned his face fully towards her and she could picture the expression on it as he said, 'You mean to say there really is a Mrs Golightly?'

'I've told you!'

'Then why is it nobody knows about her? Miss Braithwaite said she's never known anyone of that name.'

'Miss Braithwaite knows nothin'. Miss Talbot used to come and talk to her and about me. She used to give Miss Talbot a cup of tea . . . You still don't believe me?'

'Yes, yes, Bella, I do now. Yes, I do, and you know something, my father believes you, he said he did, but I thought it was just the drink talking.'

'There you see ... people think I 'magine things all because of Gip, but he's the only 'maginary one I made up, 'cos I always wanted a dog; or a cat would have done, but me da wasn't for it. Animals need looking after, he said. But when Gip came I didn't mind anymore ... well, not all that much.'

When he slowly slid his arm about her shoulders and pulled her close to him, she made a little murmuring sound but didn't speak.

And like this they stayed for quite some time, speaking only now and again. That was, until the creaking sound of the key being turned came to them once more and they swung around on the straw and peered in the direction of the stairs. Then they became rigid as a voice said in a low growling tone, 'Aw, come on. It's got to be done. Let's get it over with. And don't worry, I'll take the girl. Why you should be feared of a blind kid puzzles me ...'

There was the sound of a foot grating on the stone steps; then another voice, full of agitation now, exclaimed, 'Hold your hand a minute, Charlie. Look, there's the boss coming onto the drive an' a crowd with him. Come away back in, man, and shut the flamin' door.'

There now came to them the sound of the door being banged closed, and the echo of it had hardly died away before Bella cried, 'They're coming! They're coming lookin' for us! It'll be me granda. He's believed about the man being tied up ... Come on! Come on! Let's go up to the door and bang on it and yell.'

Before she had finished speaking she grabbed

his hand and began to grope her way to where she imagined the stairs were, and having come to the side of them, she quickly led him around to the foot. Then they were scrambling upwards, and when they reached the door they thumped on it and yelled their loudest.

They yelled and yelled until their throats were sore, and when almost simultaneously they stopped, they leaned against the door and, their hands groping towards each other now, they again almost simultaneously said, 'They can't hear us.'

After a while they moved cautiously into the blackness and down the steps again, then groped their way to the bed of straw. Sitting down, neither of them said a word for almost five minutes. Then Bella, in a small voice, whispered, 'The place must be so secret that no one knows it's here.'

'Secret! Of course! Of course! Yes.' John had suddenly risen to his feet. 'Why didn't I think about it before. This is the place old John Kepple used to talk about – he's dead now. They said he was silly, daft; he was a bit but not all that daft. He said there was a secret cellar but he had forgotten how to get into it, that's if he had ever known. It was his father who had worked here when the manor was really a manor. Anyway, it was old John who set me looking for it during the holidays. I used to go round tapping the upstairs walls and the staircase mostly. But I did try downstairs, too, but as I've told you there were no cellars.'

'Well, isn't this a cellar?'

'Yes, but it's different. Old Kepple said the house was built in the time of the Troubles – the religious troubles – and that the secret place wasn't only used for priests and later highwaymen and smugglers, but errant wives and it was a . . .' He stopped himself from adding, 'place of no return' and ended, 'a place that should be forgotten.'

After making this statement he realized its inference and became silent, and Bella didn't break the silence.

6

Joseph Dodd had been held up. It was fifteen minutes past five o'clock when he returned home, and he saw to the horse before going into the house. After glancing around the living room and the scullery, he went to the foot of the stairs and called sharply, 'You, Bella!'

When there was no reply he pressed his lips together, and jerked his chin first to one side and then the other before going up the stairs, his hobnailed boots hitting each stair as if he meant to kick it through.

As he thrust open the small bedroom door he began, 'When I call . . .' then he stopped, stared towards the bed for a moment, and turned to go banging down the stairs again, saying as he reached the bottom, 'Drat the child! I told her to be back by three, didn't I?' He addressed the remark to his high-backed wooden chair and glared at it as if daring it to contradict him.

Back in the yard, without apparent hesitation he walked towards the wood, and marched through it until he came to the broken wall. There was no sign at either side of it.

His face was livid with temper when once more he stood inside the living room. Wait until she put in an appearance. He'd make her aware once and for all that when he gave an order he meant that order to be carried out! She had been asking for a scudded backside since the first day she came, and by God! she'd get it today.

He now thrust the black kettle into the heart of the fire, brought the teapot from the hob, then went into the scullery and snatched up a tin mug from the draining board.

It wasn't until after he had brewed his tea and sat sipping the sweet scalding liquid that his temper subsided just a trifle and, turning his head, he gazed about the room. And in this moment it was as if he had never seen it before, for although it was packed with furniture, it now appeared to him empty, cold.

Where was she, anyway? He got up abruptly to his feet. Look at the time! Ten to six by the mantel clock.

He started when there came a knock on the door, and when he saw Harry Thompson standing there, his jaw stiffened.

Harry's voice was quiet with just the slightest note of anxiety in it. 'I . . . just called to see if my boy was here,' he said.

'Your boy here? What would your boy be wanting here? I was for coming along to you to see if the child was with you.'

'She's not in?'

'Would I be coming along to you to see you if she was in? Talk sense, man!'

Harry lowered his head for a moment, bit on his lip, and said patiently, 'If John is going anywhere that will take him some little time, he always leaves me a note. I got back in the house just after three; it is now six and he hasn't returned. All I wanted to know was if he was here.'

'Well, he's not here. Neither is she. The pair of them have gone off somewhere, and your lad being the age he is should have had more sense.'

'He has sense, plenty of it.' Harry's tone was brusque. 'That's why I'm worried. He has certain chores to do, special ones around four o'clock. He's never missed them yet.'

The two men now stared at each other until Joseph Dodd in a slightly mollified tone said, 'They've likely gone down to the shore, and . . . and once that young 'un starts talking, time slips by.'

'I've been down to the shore.'

Joseph blinked rapidly, then muttered, 'You have?'

'Yes, there's no sign of them there. There were some people on the beach and I enquired if they had seen anything of them but they said no, and they had been there since dinner time.'

'Have you been to the village?'

'Not as yet. I'm on my way there now. But John doesn't often go into the village, not unless he has to.' As he went to turn away, Harry Thompson paused and said, 'There's the Pictons. Their lads had a go at John last week.'

'I've just come over from their place. Their two scallywags were up to their necks in charcoal, so to speak. The old man had kept them at it all day.'

'I'll call on me way back.'

'Very good.'

They nodded at each other, then Joseph turned indoors again. He flopped down in his chair and, his hands gripping the wooden arms, his body made a slight swaying movement as if

119

he were rocking himself. Of a sudden he had a dreadful feeling on him. What if something had happened to her! But what could happen to her if she was with the lad? But what if something had happened to them both!

Aw! He now wriggled himself back into the chair and tossed his head impatiently. Fancies. Fancies. What had likely happened was that she had got talking to the boy and kept on talking and so inveigled him into taking her for a walk over the fells. Anything, he supposed, to keep her clear of this house and himself.

He became still in the chair; then his voice a mere whisper, he said aloud, 'But I haven't been hard on her ... not really. Shout, aye, I've shouted at her. But I've fed her well, and ... and I've put up with her chatter ...'

Again he was looking around the room. If anything had happened to her his life would become an empty shell. He had thought it was empty before, but if she were never to return, the whole world would become a void and he would be lost in it.

In the name of God, what was the matter with him!

He was on his feet now and making for the door when he was again startled by a rapping on it, a loud rap this time.

When he opened it he stood staring at the fat, bright-faced woman before him. She looked to him like something that had dropped out of a picture book printed in the early part of the century. She was wearing a long black coat that showed at its neck the collar of a striped blouse. On her head was a flat straw hat that had once been blue, but was now a dusty shade of grey, and the watered ribbon around its band had even faded to a dingy white in parts.

'Hello there. You Mr Dodd?'

'Yes, I'm Mr Dodd.'

'Aw well, I'm pleased to see you. I never thought I'd get here. Just a step, she said, from the cottage. A mile if it's an inch. Me feet's killin' me. I'll come in a minute and sit down.'

He effectively blocked her entrance by thrusting his arm out in front of her and growling, 'Who are you, anyway?'

'Me name's Golightly, Mrs Golightly.'

'What did you say?'

'I said me name's Golightly.'

'*Golightly!*' His voice sounded like an echo to a far call.

'Yes, that's what I said, Golightly. Are you deaf? Now if you'll just let me in an' I can get off me feet for a minute . . .'

He lowered his arm, turned his body to the side, and watched the strange bundle of clothes wobble towards the table and slowly lower itself down into a chair.

As he just as slowly moved towards her, Mrs Golightly let out a long sigh and, turning her head, she cocked her eyes up at him, saying, 'So you're Joe Dodd. Well! well! well! So you're the grandpa. Well! well! well!'

'*Golightly?*'

Mrs Golightly now narrowed her eyes and leaned forward in the chair, saying slowly, 'What's wrong with you? It's me name . . . Golightly. Surely you haven't to keep repeating it in order to remember it. It's not a common name, Golightly. Anyway' – she looked around her – 'where's the child?'

'The child?'

'In the name of God, must you keep repeatin' things! First Golightly, and now the child. Yes, Bella, you know, the little girl.' She now measured about three feet from the ground with her hand. 'Bella, Bella Dodd, who I've been given to understand has been stayin' with you for weeks past. An' if you're not any better for her company, then all I can say is there must be something wrong with you, for as I've said afore, an' to her little face, she's joy unconfined . . . What's wrong with you?'

Joseph was now sitting in his chair staring at her, and his voice was unusually quiet as he said, 'There's been a misunderstanding.'

'A misunderstanding? What kind of a misunderstanding?'

'I . . . I didn't believe you were real.'

'Ho-ho, begod!' Her head went back now and she let out a high rollicking laugh. 'I'm real, all right. Just look at me. What made you think I wasn't real?'

'Well, she . . . she imagines things. A dog called Gip and a horse called Ironsides.'

'Well now, every child imagines an animal they haven't got, it's only natural. As for Ironsides, he's as real as me. He's at the Blind School for the bairns to ride on.'

Joseph now stared at her for a moment before he said, 'How was it that the social woman knew nothing about you?'

'The social woman does know something about me, the real one, Miss Talbot. I've known her for years, but the Braithwaite one, I've seen nothin' of her or her of me. Yet that's understandable for they shifted me out of me flat and placed me in what they call ... more suitable accommodation. But they can have it. It's people that matter to me; not an indoor toilet or a bath. Broke me neck, I nearly have, twice, steppin' in and out of the thing. The bottom's like a skating rink. Put rubber on it, they said, the piece from off the draining board. Put rubber on it yourself, I said. It's not seein' neither hilt nor hair of me again. I've washed in me tin dish for sixty years and it'll see me out. Anyway, enough of this blather. Where is she? I'm just dying to see her. An' wait till she hears me voice! She'll leap from that door, I'm tellin' you, right into me arms. Aw, begod! I missed her. I never thought I'd miss anybody so much in me life; but aw, I missed her.'

'She's out.'

'Out? Where?'

'That's what I'd like to know.' He was on his feet now, and his voice had regained its natural tone. 'She's got pally with a lad along the road. He's going on fifteen, a decent enough lad, sensible.' He nodded at her. 'Well, they've both gone off somewhere. His father was here only a few minutes afore you, looking for him, and now he's searching for them both.'

'Aw, if she's with him she'll come to no harm. She knows her way about. She sees more in her darkness than we do in our daylight. She's special, that child. Do you know that? She's special. Don't you think so?'

He stared down at her for a moment now before growling, 'She's a prattler, I'll say that much for her, she's a prattler.'

'Well' – she again looked around the room – 'I should have thought you would have enjoyed that, stuck as you are out alone here in the

123

wilderness.' She now looked towards the fire, adding, 'I'm as dry as a kipper that's been over-smoked. Is there any tea in that pot?'

The look he cast down on her was almost a glare before he marched to the fireplace and lifted the stewing teapot from the hob, then went into the scullery and returned with another tin mug. When he placed it on the table, Mrs Golightly picked it up and looked at it. She looked inside, she turned it upside down and looked at the bottom, and then she said one word: 'Tin.'

'Yes, tin.'

'Haven't you a decent cup and saucer in the house?'

His lips pressed tightly together for a moment before, thrusting his arm out towards an old Dutch cupboard that stood in the corner of the room, he almost barked at her, 'That's full of cups and saucers, good china! But I'm not having them used and broken.'

Mrs Golightly raised her eyebrows while at the same time pulling down her upper lip. Looking at him with a sort of innocent expression, she said quietly, 'Well, if you don't want them ever to be broken, you'd better leave word for them to be buried with you.'

'Woman! I want none of your skit. I didn't ask you here and I'll thank you to be gone.'

Neither his manner nor his tone seemed to have any effect on Mrs Golightly for, opening the three top buttons of her coat, she wafted a lapel under her chin as if to give herself air, then said quietly, 'I came to see the child and I won't go till I've done just that; and then I hope to see her the morrow and the next day too.'

'Tomorrow and the next day? Where are you staying?'

'I'm stayin' with me friend in her cottage. Mrs Campbell, if you would like to know.'

'*You* a friend of Mrs Campbell?'

For the first time Mrs Golightly's manner took on the offensive and she cried at him, 'Yes, I'm a friend of Mrs Campbell, and she's pleased to call me so. You should never judge the parcel by its wrapper. I've got me friends in many different walks of life; an' if you're judgin' people on looks, I'd advise you never to go in front of a mirror.'

They were glaring at each other, and Joseph's eyes were the first to drop away.

Going to the delft rack, he took up a jug of milk and brought it to the table, and after banging it down in front of her he went abruptly to the door and out into the yard. She turned her head and looked over her shoulder towards the door as she muttered to herself, 'Like father, like son. Now I can see what made Davy like he was. There's something to be said for him after all, God rest his soul.'

7

It was safe to say that the yard had never seen so much activity since the day Joseph Dodd had brought his bride back to this house in which he had been born. The yard had been packed with people that day, and now here it was again packed with people.

Besides Mr Dodd and Harry Thompson, there were Farmer Pollock and one of his men. There was Dave Seaton, the blacksmith, Bill MacKay, the hated stationmaster, Mr Samson, the policeman, besides Billy Tyson, who was Lord Committy's odd job man. There were the two Picton boys and their father, and numerous villagers of all ages.

'What we've got to do is to divide up.' It was Harry speaking. 'If you, Dave, and you, Bill, and Mr Picton and the lads will take the moor, that will be best, I think, because you're well acquainted with that area.'

'We've been all over there, Mr Thompson.'

It was young Pat Picton speaking, and Harry replied, 'I know, I know. But there's gullies and gorse clumps and such, and . . . and it'll soon be dark.'

'Right, we'll be away.' It was the blacksmith who now took charge of his small group, saying, 'Come on! Come on along with me.'

'And you, Billy.' Harry was speaking to Lord Committy's man when he happened to turn and look towards the gate where Mrs Campbell was coming through almost at a run. He waited for her to approach him before going on, and it was to her he spoke, saying, 'It's all right now, it's all right.'

'I've just heard . . .'

'Go on indoors.' He pointed towards the house, then jerked his head to where Joseph Dodd was standing and asked, 'Can she?' After just the slightest hesitation, Joseph made a small motion with his head and Harry repeated, 'Go on, I'll be in in a minute.'

When Mrs Campbell entered the house she was greeted immediately by Mrs Golightly, who said, 'There you are. Now don't frash yourself. Sit down and you'll hear all about it. Do you want a cup of tea?'

Mrs Campbell sat down and she stared open-mouthed at Mrs Golightly, who seemed to have taken charge of the house, for there she was in her blue serge skirt and her striped blouse, dressed as she would have been if she had been in her own kitchen, and she was pushing the kettle into the heart of the fire as if she was in the habit of doing it daily.

'They say they're lost.'

'Yes, that's what they say, lass. But how a fourteen-year-old lad and a sensible chit like she is get lost in a place like this, where you can see for miles and the houses are few and far between, God only knows. It smells fishy to me.'

'Have . . . have they been to the beach?'

'Oh, they've searched the beach, lass, they've searched the beach.'

127

'If anything were to happen to her now, I'd ... I'd...'

'Now stop it! Stop it. Don't start bubblin'.'

'I ... I can't help it. Things were difficult enough before, but now...'

As she put her handkerchief to her eyes, the door opened and Joseph Dodd entered and, looking at her, asked abruptly, 'What's the matter?' But it was Mrs Golightly who answered, saying, 'She's crying over the child, that's what's the matter.'

'Crying over the child!' Joseph walked slowly until he stood in front of Mrs Campbell and then he said abruptly, 'There'll be time enough to cry when the worst is known. Anyway, you hardly know her.'

Mrs Campbell now rose abruptly to her feet. Her head was up, her chin thrust out, yet her lips trembled as she said, 'I've known her longer than you, much, much longer.'

They glared at each other for a moment before Joseph said, 'And what are you inferrin' by that?'

There was a longer pause now before Mrs Campbell replied steadily, 'I'm inferring that I'm her mother.'

'*Now, now, now!*' It was Mrs Golightly who came hurrying around from the far side of the table and she dared to take hold of Joseph's arm, crying at him, 'Steady on with both your hand and your tongue else you'll be sorry for it. What she said is true an' you can't get over it. She's the child's mother.'

'She's ... she's no mother!' The words were brought out from between Joseph's teeth. 'No woman who could leave her bairn, and it a small

128

infant, to God and good neighbours can call herself a mother.'

'You don't know the facts of it.'

'I know what I know. You can't get over the fact that she went off and left the child because she thought Bella was going blind.'

'I didn't! I didn't!' The emphatic denial was spat at him, and now Mrs Campbell, supporting herself against the edge of the table, leaned towards him, saying, 'You know nothing about it. I was sixteen when I married your son. I was a young, silly girl, full of thoughts of reforming a drunkard. But ... but the drinking wasn't the worst – anyway I could have put up with his drinking – but he was a cruel man, thoughtless, callous, and cruel. For almost a year I had to take the child every week to the hospital, walk there through rain or shine, because what money he had he spent on drink, and ... and I became ill, mentally and physically ill. All I remember of that time was that I realized I couldn't stand any more, and I walked out. I remember walking and walking. They told me I must have walked for two days and a night, but that was many weeks after I came to my senses, or some part of them, because I went into a deep breakdown and they put me in an asylum. Yes, an asylum. And did he once come to see me? No! Never once. When I was eventually discharged I went back to him, and what did I find? I'll tell you what I found. I found a woman there, a low, common slut, and because I ordered her out of the house he gave me this.' She pointed to her lower lip where a white weal ran from the corner to almost the end of her chin. 'And that isn't the only legacy of where his fists hit me. He might have finished me off completely if Mrs Golightly there

129

hadn't intervened. Your son, Mr Dodd, was a maniac when in drink. Do you know he went to prison for three months for what he did to me? And what would have happened to the child God only knows if it hadn't been for Mrs Golightly. And she can verify every word I am saying.'

'Yes, I can that; and I could add more to it if you want to hear.'

Joseph turned his head slowly and glared at Mrs Golightly. Then, as slowly, his gaze came to rest once more on the young woman who called herself Mrs Campbell. And now she was talking again, rapidly. 'From what I gathered, prison must have had a sobering effect on him,' she said, 'for he cut down on his drinking and looked after the child to the best of his ability. I must say that for him. I understand that when they wanted to take her into care he fought to keep her. But that's the only thing in his favour for, after the beating up, I had another breakdown and he would have left me to rot in the asylum if it hadn't been for my aunt. She was a woman whom I hadn't seen much of when I was a child. My mother died the first year I was married and when my aunt came to her funeral and saw the type of man that I'd taken for a husband she withdrew what interest she might have had in me; that was until she heard of my predicament. She then came to the hospital and took on the responsibility of me and my recovery. She was a wonderful woman.'

Mrs Campbell now moved her head, looked downwards and shook it slowly before she went on, 'She even understood when I wanted to come back to Fellburn to be close to the child. It was she who suggested that I should dye my hair and change my way of dressing to a much older style,

130

and this I did. For eighteen months I worked in Fellburn and lived within a stone's throw of the child and your son. Only one person knew of my identity' – she now turned her head towards Mrs Golightly before looking back at Joseph and saying – 'and when your son died I would have stepped in and claimed custody of the child there and then but for the fact that my aunt had also died. I had been with her during the last days of her illness and afterwards had to stay on and see to the settling up of her affairs. And that's the whole story except that I am telling you here and now, I mean to have her. She's my child and nothing will stop me from . . .'

'We'll see about that.' Joseph's words were flat, and she came back at him swiftly, saying, 'You have no claim whatever. You can do nothing.'

'Don't tell me I can do nothing . . .'

'Be quiet, the both of you! And stop a minute and think. There mightn't be any need for either of you to do anything if she's not found or found in time, so I'd make an effort, the pair of you, to gag your threats until such time . . .'

'What did you say?'

Mrs Golightly now dropped her head to the side and, staring at Joseph, she said, 'You've got the irritating habit, mister, of either repeatin' things or askin' the road you know. You heard what I said.'

'Yes, I heard what you said.'

'Then why pretend that you didn't?'

'Gag.'

'Gag? . . . Now you've got me doing it.'

'I'm thinking . . . that word, gag. She came at me this morning, the child, all flurried and bothered. She said she had gone over the wall at the bottom of the wood' – he thumbed towards the door – 'after I'd warned her not to. But she had wanted to pick flowers and while at it she said she came across a man whose mouth was gagged . . . aye, gagged, and his eyes were bandaged, and when she unloosened them he told her to go and tell her parents.'

'Name of God! And you're just tellin' us now?'

'Yes, I'm just tellin' you now. But I told Harry Thompson earlier on, and a number of us went around there. We even spoke to the owner, that Mr Aimsford, and he laughed his head off. He said she had a career all mapped out for herself for she had the main essential of a writer, a vivid imagination.' He now put his hand to his head and ran his fingers through his hair as he muttered to himself, 'She was so sure, positive, she took me back and she swore she wasn't making it up. And then there was you.' He now stabbed his index finger towards Mrs Golightly. 'She was right about you.'

'Who is the man next door, this Mr Aimsford?'

'He's a newcomer. Came about a month ago with a few sticks of furniture; waiting for his main stuff coming; over from Paris so I've been given to understand; going to do the place up first.' He blinked rapidly now and turned his gaze from Mrs Golightly onto Esther Campbell. 'Yes,' she said, 'that's what I heard, too, but they're also saying in the village there's been no attempt to clean the place up, although he's got two men there. One's a local man and a bit of a scamp from what I gather.'

Mrs Campbell stepped quickly back as Joseph rushed for the door. In the yard he called to Harry, who was making for the roadway accompanied by Farmer Pollock and Constable Samson, followed by Pat Picton. 'Hold your hand a minute!' he cried, and when he reached them it was to the constable he spoke, telling him of Bella's escapade of the morning.

'Well?' he finished.

'Fishy.' The constable shook his head.

'Aye, I'd say it's fishy.'

'And dangerous.'

'What do you mean, dangerous?'

'Well, dangerous in such a way that you can't burst into a man's grounds or house without a warrant.'

'You can ask to see around, can't you, you being of the force?'

'Aye, I can ask.' Constable Samson nodded. 'But what I should do first is ring the chief at Fellburn and get advice.'

'Advice be damned! I'm going along there now. Are you coming or not?'

The constable looked from one to the other, but it was Harry who answered for him, saying, 'Come on.' As they went to move away he turned and looked towards where Pat was standing some distance apart and said, 'I thought you were going with Dave Seaton and them?'

'Aw' – Pat jerked his head – 'I've . . . I've been all over that way. I've been over it twice today an' all that ground. They weren't there. And I did some yellin', too, and got no answer.'

It was as they all hurried out of the gate that the constable said scornfully, 'Trust a Picton to find an excuse to get out of anything that spells effort.'

8

Despite their realization that they were imprisoned in a cellar of which no outside people had knowledge, Bella and John had too little time in which to give way to despair before they heard the door above them being opened again.

Springing to their feet, they gripped each other tightly and were about to grope hopefully towards the stairs when a voice said, 'Stay where you are, you two! Just stay where you are. Don't open your mouths or move.'

Their hands clutched, they obeyed the order coming out of the darkness. There was a scrambling noise above them, followed by a heavy thud and the recognized sound of the grating lock, then silence, deep and thick like the blackness about them.

It was a full minute before John pulled himself away from Bella and groped to where the candle and matches were. Having found them, he lit the candle, and for a second its light appeared to him to be as bright as the sun. When he raised the candle above his head he saw that Bella was already halfway up the stairs and he hurried after her. When he reached her she was within three steps of the small landing, and he pulled her to a stop, saying, 'Wait!' With the candle held high he looked at the trussed figure lying prone across the boards. The head appeared to be swathed in bandages; the whole of the face was covered except the nostrils.

'It's the man.' His voice was a mere whisper.

Bella made no answer, but she scrambled forward and fell across the prostrate form.

'Untie his legs,' she said, pulling the gag from the man's mouth; then with a swiftness that would have outdone any sighted person, her fingers were behind his head loosening the knots of the blindfold.

'O ... oh. O ... oh.' The sound was in the nature of a groan.

'Are you all right?'

It was John who answered her, saying, 'Of course he's not all right. Here, hold the candle. I can't do anything with one hand.'

He pushed the candle into her hand, admonishing her now, 'Hold it steady. Keep it from his face. You don't want to scald him with hot grease.'

'I'm not that silly. What do you take me for?' For a moment it was the old Bella talking. But when the groans began again she said softly, 'You'll be all right. You'll be all right,' and after a pause she added, 'Why isn't he speaking? His eyes are closed.' She was touching his lids with the fingers of one hand now. 'He seems asleep.'

'Likely drugged. There, that's his legs free. I'll have to turn him on his side to get to his hands.'

The knots in the rope binding the man's hands were even tighter than those that had bound his legs, and it was some minutes before John slowly eased the prostrate form onto its back again, saying, 'We'll have to get him down the steps.'

'Try to wake him up.'

He was again about to answer, 'Don't be silly!' when he thought better of it and, taking the man by the shoulders, he attempted to shake him gently, saying, 'Mister! Mister! Wake up! Come on, wake up!'

The movement caused the man to groan again, then mutter something.

'What do you say?'

Again there came the muttering, and Bella, her ear now close to the man's mouth, whispered, 'He's saying a name . . . Margaret.'

Gently now, John pushed Bella aside, adding, 'If I can get him to sit up he might wake. Come on, mister, come on, sit up.'

'What? What, Margaret?' The words were clear now; then stronger still: 'Oh, my head.'

'That's it, mister. Don't lie down again.'

'O . . . oh! O . . . oh!'

John pulled at the man's shoulders, then again he said, 'Listen, there's steps here. I want to get you down them. If you stay here you might fall over; there's . . . there's no banister.'

'What? Oh, dear me! Oh, my head!'

'Wake up. Wake up, sir.' The sound of the man's cultured voice had changed John's mode of address.

Bending forward now of his own volition, the man linked his hands about his wrists and shook them as if trying to throw off the pain. Presently he raised his head and stretched his eyelids, then peered around him. His gaze coming to rest on Bella, who was standing two steps below him holding the candle, he drew in a number of short breaths before muttering, 'The child. The blind child.' Then turning his gaze to John, he asked in

136

an almost normal voice, 'Why . . . why are you here? What . . . what happened to you? They surely didn't . . .?'

'Yes; yes, they did, sir,' put in John now, nodding at the man. 'We were looking for you. Bella told me about you. She had told other people, but they didn't believe her, and when I found you out in the outhouses they found me, and then they caught Bella, and they pushed us in here.'

'What is it, a cellar?'

'More than that, I think, sir.'

The man put his hand to his head and groaned, and his words came slow again and muffled as he said, 'They . . . they made me drink something. I can't remember anything after they brought me into the house.'

'Do you think you can manage the steps, sir?'

'Yes. Yes.'

'You go ahead, Bella, and hold the candle high,' said John now; then turning to the man, he added, 'I would sit on the steps, sir, and bump yourself down. You won't be very steady on your legs in any case, being tied up so long.'

'Yes, yes, you're right.'

The man now inched himself forward and, assisted by John's grip on his shoulders, he made his way step by step to the bottom. But when he reached the floor of the cellar and attempted to stand, he would have fallen had not John steadied him, saying as he did so, 'We've got straw on the floor over here, sir. You'll be able to rest on it.'

When they reached the straw the man sank thankfully down onto it; then after a moment he asked, 'Have you any water?'

'No, sir, nothing.'

'They're devils!'

137

'They'll soon be caught.' Bella's words sounded emphatic, and she nodded in what she thought was their direction, adding, 'They're in a panic, that's why they dumped you in here. They were coming for us for some reason or other, weren't they, John? And then one of them shouted that there was a crowd of people coming up the drive and I knew it would be me granda and John's da and others. They'll soon find us.'

The words of comfort were cut off by John's saying, 'Don't be silly. You heard what that fellow said about this place.'

The man's voice now checked what would have been a stinging retort from Bella when he asked quietly, 'What did he say?'

'Well, sir, he seemed to suggest that this was a very secret place, sort of soundproof. The door up above just leads into a passage, and there's another wall, a thick wall.'

There was silence for a moment, and then Bella, her tone holding that anxious tremor, asked, 'What do you think they'll do to us, sir?'

'Oh, from what I've experienced of them they'll stop at nothing to ...' The man paused and seemed to consider, then said in a lighter tone, 'Oh, once the money is paid they will make their escape and likely leave word where we are to be found.'

John was quick to realize that the man was now trying to allay their fears.

'May ... may I ask who you are, sir?' John tentatively put the question, and the man answered, 'I'm Sir Geoffrey Cotton-Bailey.'

'Cotton-Bailey.' John repeated the words quietly. 'Not Cotton-Bailey, the steel works, I ... I mean, the owner of the steel works? It ... it was

138

in the papers a little while ago. You married the American heiress . . .'

'Yes, yes, the same.'

There was silence again before John said, 'They'll expect big money for you, sir?'

'Doubtless.'

'Will . . . will your people pay it?'

'Oh, they'll pay it.'

'How long is it since they took you, sir?'

'What is today?'

'It's still Friday, sir.'

'Oh well, this is the third day. They picked me up on Wednesday morning.'

'*Wednesday!*'

'Yes, Wednesday.'

'But, sir, I read this morning's paper and I listened to the news, and there wasn't a thing in there about you.'

'Oh, I'm not surprised at that; that would be one of their conditions. Notify the police or the newspapers and we finish him off, they would say. But I haven't a doubt about it but that the police are well-informed and are just biding their time . . . Oh, what I'd give for a mouthful of water.'

'I'm dry too.'

'I'm sure you are, child.' The man now put his hand out and caught hold of Bella's and, pulling her gently down beside him, he said, 'I think you're a brave little girl. You'll likely be the means of saving us all.'

'I won't, but me granda will. He'll knock stick out of 'em when he finds out what they've done.'

'Yes . . . yes, I'm sure he will.'

'I . . . I think, sir, we'd better put the candle out.'

139

'Why?'

'Well, you see, the man only left us three and this one's nearly gone.'

'Oh yes. Yes.'

When they were enveloped in darkness again, the man said softly, 'There's no light whatever down here?'

'No, sir.'

'It's a funny place altogether, like a ditch,' said Bella.

'A ditch?'

'Yes, 'cos this is the only flat bit, this bit we're sitting on. The floor slopes up under those stairs, and at the other side where the boxes are stacked it slopes up again.'

'Really!'

'She's right, sir. I never thought of it like that before but it is made like a ditch.'

'Who owns the house?'

'A man calling himself Mr Aimsford, and he seems to be the boss of this outfit. Bella recognized one of the other men, at least she made me recall him. His name is Dick Riley. He's from the village and he's been in trouble with the police before now. He goes out fishing with one of the boats along the coast . . .'

'Fishing . . . boats. I remember now: that's it, something about a boat and getting me across. Yes, yes, that's what they meant to do. And still mean to do, take me across the water somewhere. It wouldn't be Norway. No; no, that would be too evident . . .'

'What you doing, Bella? Where are you going?' It was John's voice now and she answered, 'Never you mind.'

'Oh.'

'Where's she going?' Sir Geoffrey's enquiry was soft, and after a moment's hesitation, John answered him as softly: 'To . . . to the toilet, sir.'

'Toilet?'

'Well, I mean, sir, she's gone up by the wall. There's a space up there.'

'Oh, I understand.'

Bella could hear plainly what they were saying and in her embarrassment she moved further up by the wall, her hands outstretched before her. But it wasn't what her hands found that brought her to a stop, for all of a sudden she realized that she was walking on level ground again.

When her feet were obstructed by a box, she bent down and fingered it and found that she could squeeze between it and the wall. Her hands patting the wall now, she went forward. When she was again obstructed she found that this time two boxes, one piled on top of the other, left only a narrow gap between themselves and the wall, and as she went to squeeze past them she pushed against them. This was followed by a rumbling noise and a succession of bangs, and John's voice shouting now, 'What are you up to in there? Come out, you'll have the whole lot on top of us.'

She stood still, her back pressed tightly against the wall. After a moment during which she endeavoured to get over her fright, she called back, 'It's . . . it's all right. I . . . I pushed a box.'

Her hands now searched in front of her and to the side. The way seemed to be clear but the floor was again sloping upwards and she had only gone a few short steps forward when her outstretched hand touched a further wall and she knew that she had come to the end of this place. But her

141

fingers told her there was one difference between
the wall in front of her and the wall to the side of
her: the wall to the front of her felt damp, even
wet, and its surface was scaly; as her hand moved
over it the stone flaked away under her nails. She
was about to investigate further, for she found
that once again she was standing on level ground
and apparently it wasn't obstructed by boxes,
when her sharp ears caught the sound of a grating
lock. Carefully now, she turned about and groped
her way back. She had just reached the place
where she had to squeeze between the boxes and
the wall when she recognized the voice to be that
of the man who smelled of fish, calling, 'There's a
jug of tea and some grub. I'll leave it up here for
you; come and get it. Oh, an' I know you'll be
loosened by now but that's not going to help you,
mister.'

Neither John nor the man answered, and Bella
waited until she heard the creaking of the lock
before sidling slowly forward again, to be greeted
by John's voice, saying, 'Look where you're
going! I'm lighting the candle.'

'Oh . . . Oh, I'm sorry, but John . . .'

'Shut up a minute until I get the food down.'

She now turned in what she imagined to be the
direction of where Sir Geoffrey was sitting and
said, 'Speak to me, please, then I'll know where
you are.'

'This way, dear. That's it, this way.'

She reached his side as John was coming down
the stairs carrying a tin tray on which was a plate
of thick slices of bread and a small mound of
pieces of cheese. Placing the tray on the floor, he
said, 'He's given us only one mug. I'll . . . I'll give
her a drink first, sir.'

142

'No.'

'What!'

'No, let me taste it. It was tea they gave me before and I was so thirsty I gulped at it before I realized that it had a queer tang. Just let me taste this.'

John half filled the mug with tea and handed it towards Sir Geoffrey. When after a moment he said, 'It's the same. You mustn't drink it,' John visibly slumped. His mouth was so dry he was finding it difficult to swallow; what was more, the air in the cellar seemed to be getting fuggier.

'I'm sorry, my dear.' Sir Geoffrey was addressing Bella, and she answered, 'So am I, because like Mrs Golightly used to say, me mouth feels like an oversmoked kipper.'

'Mrs Go . . .?'

'It's a lady she knows, sir, who is always coming out with odd sayings.'

'Oh . . . oh, I understand.'

'Can we eat the bread then and whatever they've sent down?'

'Yes, I think we can safely eat that. They would imagine we'd gulp at the tea first.'

After taking a few mouthfuls of the bread and cheese and swallowing deeply to get it down her throat, Bella said casually, 'There's a wall up there and it's rotten.'

'What?' Both John and Sir Geoffrey spoke together.

'Up behind the boxes. There's two levels, not as broad as this one, just sort of ledges, and then the floor slopes up again. But the wall's all crumbly and wet. If we had a hammer or something, we could likely knock a hole through.'

'A hammer or something?' Sir Geoffrey had

143

now risen to his feet and for a moment he swayed, then put his hand to his head as he said, 'I'm still not clear of it. But ... but come on, my dear, show me. Will you hold the candle, boy?' He turned to John and added, 'What is your name?'

'John Thompson, sir.'

'Well, John, let's see what she's found. But wait. Let's see if there's any implement lying around.'

Holding the candle high, John walked around the enclosed space, then said, 'There's nothing that I can see, sir, but I've got a penknife on me.'

'A penknife? Well, all I can say at this moment is thank God for boys and penknives. I only hope it's a stout one.'

'It's pretty good.'

'Come on then. And you lead the way, child.'

With her hands moving along the wall, Bella went quickly forward until she came to where the boxes blocked the path. Turning about, she said, 'We can push them aside, because if they tumble the rest over it won't matter when none of us are there, will it?'

'No. But in any case go carefully.'

When Sir Geoffrey and John went to squeeze through the narrow aperture there was another rumble from the boxes, but it was followed by only one thump, and then a sound that suggested that they were all settling comfortably into place again.

'Here, feel. It's all wet, isn't it?' Bella was now tapping the wall.

'Yes, yes, at least this part is.' Sir Geoffrey was moving his hands over the wall now. 'Yet to the side it's dry. And ... and the wall to the left is dry too!'

144

'Let me try with my knife, sir. Here, you hold the candle.' He now pushed the candle into Bella's hand; then gripping the knife in his fist, he inserted it between the stones. When the damp mortar splayed out almost as soft as when it had first been placed there, he laughed excitedly as he said, 'The mortar's rotten, sir. We could have the stones out of here in no time.'

'It's too good to be true. Here, let me have a try.'

Sir Geoffrey now grabbed the knife from John and started frantically digging the mortar from between the stones; but in a very short time he began to tire and, putting his hand to his head again, he muttered, 'Damn!'

'Give it here, sir.' Again John had the knife, and when he had loosened the fourth side of one stone and was about to put his hand flat on it and push it outwards, Sir Geoffrey checked him hastily, saying, 'Don't let it fall. It might drop into the open and give the show away. This wet patch has likely been caused by a blocked gutter.'

'Yes, yes, you're right, sir.' Now wedging his fingers about the stone, John edged it forward, and when he went to lift it from its place its weight nearly bent him double, and it took all his strength to hold it and not let it drop onto the concrete floor. Now both he and Sir Geoffrey had their eyes to the hole, and it was John who said, 'There's no daylight, sir.'

'No.'

'Give me the candle, Bella.' He turned and took the candle from Bella's hand, and when he put it into the place where the stone had been he whispered in disappointment, 'There's some obstruction across the middle here. We'll have to take out the upper stones before we can see further.'

'Wait a minute.' Bella was sniffing loudly, and it was she who now said, 'Hold the candle, will you?' When John took it from her she asked, 'Where's the hole?'

'Here.' Sir Geoffrey brought her face on a level with the aperture, and still sniffing, she said, 'Coal an' coke.'

'Coal and coke; what do you mean?'

She turned her face towards John, saying, 'There's coal an' coke in there. I can smell it. It must be a coalhouse.'

'Eeh! Bella.' There was an unstinted note of admiration in John's voice, and now he added, 'Well, if it's a coalhouse, let's get into it as quickly as possible. What do you say, sir?'

'I was never in more agreement with anyone in my life, John. The coalhouse seems to be our only avenue of escape. If Bella hadn't found that damp mortar I think our chances of getting out would have been pretty slim.'

John was about to start his gouging of the mortar again when Bella said quietly, 'What if they come back and expect to find us all laid out with that drink?'

John stopped his activity and there was silence for a moment before Sir Geoffrey said softly, 'My dear, your wits are much clearer than mine. You've certainly got something there.' Then, addressing John, he said, 'Do you think from the time they put the key in that lock we'd be able to scramble back onto that straw and pretend to be asleep?'

'I doubt it, sir.'

146

'If you could do it in ten seconds you'd make it,' said Bella.

'Ten seconds?'

'Yes.' Bella had turned in the direction of Sir Geoffrey. 'I've got to count things, like the time it takes for an egg to boil. Me da used to like his done for four minutes, and I used to count sixty seconds four times. You do it like this: hundred and one, hundred and two, hundred and three. The hundred gives you your timing. I do it for all kinds of things even when I don't know I'm doing it. I remember doing it the second time the man opened the door.'

'Child, you're a genius.' Sir Geoffrey squeezed her chin and it stopped her from telling him what Mrs Golightly said she was on such an occasion as now when she used her wits. John said quickly, 'Time me. Go on back down there and when you say, 'Right!' I'll make a dash for it and see if I can do it.'

A few minutes later her voice came to them, saying, 'Right!'

Turning from the wall, John scrambled downwards, only to lose his sense of direction in the dark as soon as he reached the lower level. Yet as Bella was saying, 'Nine,' he flung himself down and lay prone, and she called to him, 'You've done it!'

'Where am I?' He put out his hand gropingly, and she went towards him, caught hold of him, and said, 'The wall's here.'

When he reached it he looked upwards into the glimmer of the candlelight that was almost hidden by the boxes.

Now making his way back up again, he took the candle from Sir Geoffrey and said, 'It can be done.'

'Yes, you can do it but I doubt if I'll make it.'

147

Bella's voice came to them now, calling, 'Right!' which set Sir Geoffrey scrambling down by the wall. But he had managed to reach only the beginning of the level when she said, 'Ten,' and on his exclamation she called to him, 'Well, it doesn't matter where you're lying as long as they can see you, does it?'

'No, my dear, I don't suppose it does. But John must come first, otherwise I'll hold him up.'

'Yes, that's right. And you must pour the tea out.'

'Yes, we must pour the tea out.'

Sir Geoffrey gave a short laugh and Bella knew he was shaking his head. She said to him, 'I'd better stay here then?'

'Yes, my dear.' There was a pause now before he asked, 'You're . . . you're not frightened?' only to add quickly, 'That was a silly thing to ask.'

'No, no, it wasn't, though I'm not as frightened as I was. I was scared stiff when I first came down, but you don't get so frightened when you're doing things; it's when you're sittin' and thinkin'. Mrs Golightly used to say that eggs hatched with heat, and fear hatched with idleness.'

'She must be a very wise woman, this Mrs Golightly.'

'Yes, she is.'

'I must go now and help John.'

'Mister.'

'Yes?'

'What if when we're pretending to be asleep they pick us up and carry us away?'

It was as if he hadn't heard her question, so long did he take to answer it; and then he said, 'Yes, what if? Well, my dear, I think in that case John and I'll put up a fight.'

'I'm good at fightin' meself once I get a hold.'

She smiled in her darkness as she heard the man give a low chuckle, then say, 'I'm sure you'd be good at anything you attempted, my dear.'

He was a nice man. She liked him.

When Sir Geoffrey reached John, he exclaimed excitedly, 'Oh, you've got another two out, that's good.'

'The mortar's rotten and it's just the lifting of them out now. But it'll take us to hurry for this candle is half gone. That's another thing, sir. We must remember to snuff this out should Bella give us the warning.'

'Yes, indeed. That child, she's remarkably intelligent.'

John puffed as he lifted another stone out of the wall, then said, 'She's got her wits about her.'

Sir Geoffrey now bent down to the hole that John had made and he asked quietly, 'Do you think you could get your head and shoulders through there now?'

'I'll try, but I've got to put my arm through first to hold the candle, because it looks as black in there as it is in here.'

Taking the candle now from where he had stuck it on a protruding stone, he pushed his arm through the aperture, then slowly edged his head and shoulders after it; but it was only a matter of seconds before he withdrew it again, saying excitedly, 'It's as she said, it's a coalhouse. There's a heap of coal against one wall and nothing else. There's a door, but it looks heavy and it'll likely be barred on the outside . . . What do you think we should do?'

'Nothing at present, for I feel sure they'll come to inspect us in a short while. What I think we

149

should do now is to go back and take up our positions on the floor to be . . .'

'*Right!*'

The next second they were in blackness and John was scrambling through it, his hands clutching at the wall. When he reached the straw and threw himself down, he knew that Bella was already there. But what he didn't know was whether or not Sir Geoffrey had made it.

He felt Bella's hand pressing into the middle of his back, and through it he felt her trembling.

And Bella *was* trembling. She told herself to try to stop it but she couldn't; even her teeth seemed to be rattling in her head. She heard two sets of footsteps coming down the stairs now. She heard them stop at the foot of the stairs, then one set of steps coming towards her.

Her knuckles pressed tighter into John's spine as she felt the presence near her. Then a voice said, 'Dead to the world.' The footsteps moved away. Then the voice came to them from the far end of the cellar, saying now, 'He must have passed out where he stood, and he would, too, right on top of the other dose.'

Bella's whole body tensed further now as she listened to the second voice, the gentleman's voice, saying, 'It should keep them quiet until dawn. By that time we should have him aboard. We've got to have him aboard. Do you hear, Riley?'

'I hear, but it's gonna be easier said than done, for as I said, it's me opinion they'll be out lookin' for the pair of them. An' why do you want to take him across the water anyway? Isn't this place secret enough?'

'You're a fool, Riley. Even a rabbit has two

150

holes to its burrow. This place is only secret as long as they don't get wind of it. But I found it, didn't I? I found it through listening to tales, old men's tales, and it only needs someone to start one of the old villagers talking again and we'd have need of that other hole. I can smell trouble a mile off. I first got a whiff of it when I ran into that nosy, pert little individual.'

'I say again, I think it's a crazy idea.'

'It's the only one that'll work. I'll let them see me driving out of the village on my own. I'll stop to make enquiries about the children. I'll make it known that I'm on my way to Newcastle, but that I'll be back at first light to help them in their search.'

They were going up the stairs now and the voice of the 'fishy man', as she thought of Dick Riley, came to her, saying, 'It'll be no easy job carryin' a dead weight for a quarter of a mile, an' in the black dark.'

'There'll be three of you when Morton gets here to tell us the boat's ready. And it's not a quarter of a mile, it's just across the road and over the field. As I said, I'll be waiting at yon end with the car.'

'What if we bump into poachers?'

'Poachers? Huh! I understood that you, Benbow, and Morton were the leaders in that game around here.'

'Aw.'

The voices faded away; the key grated in the lock.

'Nosy, pert little individual, indeed!' Bella muttered angrily. She went to move but John's hand, coming quickly behind him, prevented her. It was almost a full minute before he released the pressure on her. Then when Sir Geoffrey's voice came in a muted whisper, saying, 'All right?' John answered as softly, 'All right.'

The next minute the three of them were close together touching each other, and Sir Geoffrey whispered, 'I don't know how long we've got but I think we'd better get through there as quickly as possible and see what we can do with that door.'

'May I come now?'

'Yes, of course, my dear. In fact, we'll rely on you to lead the way. First of all, can you find that other candle and the matches?'

'Yes, I think so. If I was standing at the bottom of the stairs, I . . . I could tell you where John put them.'

She drew away from him and groped forward, and when she came in contact with the wall she turned to her right until she reached the foot of the stairs. Taking her bearings from there, she began to move parallel with the bottom step. When suddenly she bumped into John she gave a small laugh and said, 'They should be just a few paces behind you.'

A minute later John said, 'She's right, here they are.' When he had lit the last candle he went towards the further wall, and Sir Geoffrey followed him, holding Bella by the hand now.

Here they worked furiously enlarging the hole, but as time went on, the work became harder. They were digging into partly dried mortar now, for as Sir Geoffrey had pointed out to John, they had better not loosen any more of those stones that led towards the roof because, the support gone, this whole section might drop.

152

John scraped frantically at the mortar around the big stone that would enable not only himself and Bella to make their escape from the cellar, but also Sir Geoffrey, who, although apparently of slim build, had broad shoulders.

'There.' Between them they eased the stone from its resting place and onto the ground.

'Now here goes.' John looked from Sir Geoffrey to Bella. The next minute he went head first through the hole; then when he was on his feet again he took the candle that Sir Geoffrey was holding out and, securing it hastily to the floor near his feet, he put out his arms and helped to ease Bella through the jagged aperture.

Next came Sir Geoffrey. But his entry into the coalhouse wasn't to be so easy as theirs, for he found that his shoulders became wedged. Whispering hoarsely now, he said, 'I'll try feet first.'

To support himself he gripped at the stones above his head, only to have John warn, 'Careful, sir! They're loose. You could bring them down.'

'I'll take my coat off. It'll give me another inch or so.'

After the whispered words he again thrust his head through the hole, and now, drawing his shoulders inwards, he pressed himself forward. At one point he gave a stifled groan as the jagged edge of stone tore through his shirt and scraped his flesh; but then with a heave, and as if he had been popped like a cork from a bottle, he came sprawling onto the floor of the coalhouse.

Remaining on his hands and knees for a moment, his head bent forward, he gave a shaky laugh. And when he felt Bella's hands on him and her voice enquiring anxiously, 'You all right, mister?' he said, 'Yes, I'm all right, child.'

John now helped him to his feet, and he, too, gave a shaky laugh as he said, 'It's like as if you'd just come up from the pits, sir; you're all coal dust.'

'You want to see *yourself*, John.'

They smiled weakly at each other in the candlelight. Then John went to the door and turned the handle gently, and not so gently he tried to pull the door towards him, but without effect.

Speaking over his shoulder, he muttered, 'It won't budge. It must be locked on the outside, and it's a stout door.'

Sir Geoffrey nodded, saying now, 'We're no better off.'

'There's fresh air coming from somewhere near here.'

They both turned towards where Bella was standing beside the heap of coal, and almost running across the short distance towards her now, they both looked upwards. Then John, turning and grabbing up the candle from the floor, held it high above his head as he exclaimed excitedly, 'It's a coal hatch! A round coal hatch. It's like a grate. If only we could get up there.'

'Could you reach it from my shoulders?'

John turned and looked at Sir Geoffrey and said slowly, 'I doubt it, sir, unless you stood on something.'

'There's the coal,' said Bella.

They both turned towards her, and it was John who answered, saying, 'But it's in the wrong place, too far to the side. They've used the coal that was under the hatch first.'

'Well, you can move it, can't you?'

It was the kind of tone that John associated with her, and under other circumstances he

154

would have retorted in kind, but now, his voice flat, he said, 'We haven't a shovel or anything.'

'We can use our hands. Mrs Golightly used to say . . .'

'Oh, be quiet! Anyway, you haven't seen this lot. It doesn't look very much, but it'll take some moving.'

'Well' – her voice was tart – 'I don't mind gettin' me hands dirty, even if you do. Will you show me, mister, which way you want the pieces put?'

As Sir Geoffrey made a little sound in his throat, John said, 'Aw, you! You always put people in the wrong.'

'I don't. That's not fair.'

There was a pause before John, turning to Sir Geoffrey, said, 'I'm sorry, sir.'

'Don't be sorry. It sounded so normal.'

'Yes, yes, it did, didn't it? John gave one of his rare chuckles, then added magnanimously, 'You're . . . right, Bella. We've got our hands and we'd better start now. Here' – he pulled her towards him – 'move what you can to your right. Take two steps and put them down there.' He directed her. 'Get it?'

'Yes. Yes.'

Scrambling now, she started to pick up the pieces of coal but Sir Geoffrey's voice halted her, saying, 'Lay them down quietly, dear; you don't know who might be in the yard.'

'Oh yes. Yes. Aye.'

'I'd forgotten about that.' John nodded his head.

For what seemed to all of them like a long night they kept lifting pieces of coal, walking two steps and putting them down, until at last John, looking at the pile, said, 'That's almost the lot. I

155

think it might be big enough now. But there's one thing, sir.'

'Yes, what's that, John?'

'When we go to stand on the top of it, it'll likely splay out a bit.'

'Yes, there's a point there, it may give. But anyway, we're got to try. Here goes.'

Sir Geoffrey began to clamber up the pile of coal, but as he did so it gave way immediately under his feet, so that when he stood on the top of it he was moved to say ruefully, 'We're going to lose half the height. But come on, try.' He held out his hand and John gripped it, then was standing by his side.

'Can you climb up my back?' said Sir Geoffrey now. 'I'd better not bend because I don't know whether I'll be able to straighten up with you on it. You'll be no light weight.'

As John tried to carry out this manoeuvre the coal slithered away still further. When at last he was astride Sir Geoffrey's shoulders he felt him sway perilously for a moment. 'Steady, sir. Steady,' he said.

One thing he was certain of now and that was he would be unable to balance on Sir Geoffrey's shoulders. Were he even to attempt it he could see them both tumbling down to the floor.

'I'm . . . I'm going to raise my arms now, sir. Do you think you can hold me steady?'

'I'm . . . I'm doing my best. The coal is not exactly acting like a platform.'

John made no retort to this but slowly now he stretched his arms upwards towards the grid, and he felt a thrill almost like joy running through him as his fingers touched the slatted iron. But that's all they did; they could only touch the iron. He couldn't stretch his hand far enough to get the palm flat on the grid and push it upwards. Three times he made the effort, then panting, he said, 'I'm . . . I'm just a few inches short, sir.'

'You should stand on a box.' They both became motionless at the sound of Bella's hissed whisper. Neither of them answered her, but John, suddenly sliding down from Sir Geoffrey's shoulders, ran across to the hole and within a minute he was through it. Another minute and he was pushing a wooden box into Sir Geoffrey's hands. When he was once again standing in the cellar he said excitedly, 'That should do it. And it's strong, it'll hold you. It must have been for something heavy because it's wired at the bottom. Turned upside down like this, it should do the trick.'

'Let's hope I can do the trick and stand on it. I think it's going to be more difficult for me to balance on that than it was on the coal because on the coal one's feet had some purchase. Still, come on, let's try.'

John stared at Sir Geoffrey for a moment. He couldn't make out the expression on his face because of the coal dust, but he knew by the sound of his voice that the man was tired and weak and that the strain of his capture was telling on him.

'I'll be as quick as I can, sir.'

'I know you will, John.'

When the box was wedged firmly on top of the coal, Sir Geoffrey took his place on it; but as soon as John began to mount his shoulders he overbalanced. With one foot in the coal and one on the box he stood panting, and even his voice was unsteady now as he said, 'I . . . I don't seem to have the strength to bear you.'

'I'm not so heavy.'

Again they turned their heads and looked to where Bella was gazing sightlessly towards them.

'John could steady you and I could get on your shoulders; and I am quite strong. I've carried buckets of coal from the coalhouse up three flights. I could push that grid up once I felt it.'

Again neither of them spoke, but John bounded down the coal heap and gripped her by the hand. The next minute she was standing pressed close to Sir Geoffrey, and John was saying, 'I'll support you from the back, sir. Take her up in your arms and put her on your shoulders. She'll be able to stand on them if you hold her legs. Come on now, ready?'

Bella felt Sir Geoffrey's arms about her; she felt herself being lifted high in the air; but when her feet came to rest on Sir Geoffrey's shoulders and her legs were pressed tight against his head, she kept her body doubled for she felt she was going to fall. At this moment John's voice came at her, saying in a hushed, stiff whisper, 'Take your time. You won't fall 'cos I can catch you from the back. Now straighten up slowly and stretch your arms high above your head, a little to the front. That's it. That's it. Good. Good, Bella . . . good, you've got it.'

When Bella felt her fingers touch the iron grid she played them over the bars as if on the notes of a piano; then, her hands going through the slits, she pressed upwards, but nothing happened.

'Try again. It will be very heavy.'

As she tried again she told herself that yes, it

158

was very heavy, but hadn't she carried those buckets of coal all the way up three flights of stairs? She bent her knees slightly now and pushed, and she almost cried out aloud with excitement as she felt the grid give just the slightest bit. Again she pushed, and again; then pausing for breath, she bent her head down and whispered, 'It's moving. It's moving.'

'Take your time. Take a rest.'

She took a rest, then tried again. She tried again and again and again, and with every effort the grid moved a few inches upwards then stuck. Her hands through the grid giving her support, she leaned her head towards her arms, saying now despondently, 'It won't open, not all the way. I can't lift it up.'

'*Somebody down there?*'

Her head bounced up so quickly she almost fell backwards; then she bent it forward in the direction of Sir Geoffrey's face as she whispered, 'Was that you?'

'No. Listen.' It was John who answered.

There it came again, the voice. '*Somebody down there?*'

'It's that lad! It's that lad!' she was shouting now, and Sir Geoffrey cut in hastily, saying, 'Ssh! Ssh! Not so loud.'

Now she was whispering up towards the grid. 'You, are you the Picton lad?'

'Aye ... An' it's you. That's where you are then.'

'Pat!' John was straining his whole body upwards now. 'Pat! It's me, John Thompson. Can you lift that grid?'

'Aye, I suppose so.' It was a nonchalant answer. 'There's a bar across it. Just a minute.'

159

They all waited, their hearts thumping against their ribs; then in the dim candlelight they saw the grid being lifted upwards, and the night above seemed almost like daylight to John.

'Here, gie us your hand.'

Bella, who had been bent over and was clinging to Sir Geoffrey's head, straightened up and stretched out her hands and felt them gripped. Then the boy's voice came at her in a hoarse whisper, saying, 'Cor! I can't hold you. Look, grip the edge.'

He guided Bella's hands to the iron-rimmed edge of the coal hatch; then saying, 'Hang on tight and I'll pull you up by the shoulders,' he hauled at her.

For a moment she felt that her dress was being pulled over her head, then it caught under her arms, and as she felt the fingers digging into her shoulder blades she heaved herself upwards. Now she was kneeling, panting, on the rough flags of the yard.

Leaning down into the hole now, Pat said, 'There's two of you down there?' and John's voice came back to him, whispering, 'Yes, Sir Geoffrey Cotton-Bailey is here. They ... they kidnapped him.'

'Oh, kidnapped, eh! Eeh! What d'you know 'bout that? She was right then. Well, which of you is comin' up first?'

Back in the cellar, John said, 'I'll help you up, sir. I'll give you a push.'

'No, no. If you do that you'll not be able to get out yourself; you could never reach the grid. Get on my shoulders again.'

'No, sir.'

'Do as I bid you' – the voice was stern

160

now –'and once you're out, run and get help as fast as you can.'

'But, sir!'

'Don't argue, John. I can't reach that hole from here, neither have I the strength to try. Now if you want to be of assistance to me, get out of here and run for your lives, because I'm afraid that's just what you'll have to do. I wouldn't be answerable if those devils caught you.'

Without further ado John now climbed up the stooping back and, from kneeling on Sir Geoffrey's shoulders, he slowly brought himself upright on the now swaying figure. It was at the very moment that Sir Geoffrey's hands took their support from his legs and his shoulders seemed to melt away from beneath his feet that he made a frantic grip at the rim of the hole. As his legs thrashed frantically beneath him, Pat's hands gripped first his hair and then the collar of his coat; then they were clutching at his back. Gasping, he emerged into the open and, like Bella had, lay in a huddled heap for a moment on the ground. But when he turned to Pat and said, 'Put the top back,' Bella hissed at him, 'You're not goin' to leave him?'

'We've got to. He's too weak to get up. We've got to get help.'

Turning on his hands and knees now, he assisted Pat to put the iron grid back into place; then gripping hold of Bella's arm, he said, 'Come on.'

'No, no, not that way.' It was Pat's voice now. 'Charlie Morton has just gone in the front way. We'd better go through the copse and onto the main road.'

As John now followed Pat on tiptoe while

161

pulling Bella behind him, he whispered hoarsely, 'We'll still have to pass the gates.'

'We'll have to take our chance on that.'

The copse was almost as black dark as the cellar, but Pat seemed to be nearly as proficient as Bella at finding his way through blackness. When they emerged into the field that led to the road, he came to a halt and whispered, 'Charlie Morton wasn't going in there at this time of the night to say hello, and by now they might have found out you're missing, so if they should come on us along the road we'll have to scatter, you one way and me the other . . .'

'And leave her?'

'Aye. They won't take her again. There wouldn't be any point. They'd want you both and me an' all now.'

'I'll . . . I'll not leave her. I can't leave her.'

'He's right, John. I don't mind. You've got to get help to get the mister out of that. And anyway I'd scream me head off, and if there's anybody about in me granda's yard they'd be bound to hear. Me granda'll likely be out himself.'

'No, come on.'

Once again John was tugging her forward, and when they reached the road he said, 'We'd better walk on the grass verge,' and to this Pat said, 'Aye. Aye.'

When the iron gates leading to the manor loomed in trellised blackness the boys' steps slowed for a moment; then, as if of one mind, they sprinted forward and kept running even when they were well past the gates.

When they stopped they were breathless, and it was Pat who said on a laugh, 'Eeh! I expected them to pounce out of the gates.'

'They couldn't have found us gone.' John spoke between long drawn breaths. 'But they could be going down into the cellar any minute now. Come on, let's run. Take her hand.'

Bella found her other hand gripped and her feet hardly seemed to touch the ground until with a great surge of feeling akin to joy she felt them skipping from one uneven stone to another in her grandfather's yard.

9

Joseph sat in his high-backed chair. His back was straight, his hands were gripping the arms, his eyes were wide open. Slowly he moved his gaze around the room; in the soft glow of the lamp his eyes skimmed over the occupants. Harry Thompson, his elbows on the table, his head resting in his cupped palms; next to him Jack Pollock and Dave Seaton, each sipping at a mug of tea. They had just returned from another fruitless search and were thankful for the warm drink before making for home to wait until daylight when, as they said, they would start again.

Then Joseph's eyes came to rest on the two women sitting on the couch. The fat, chattering old woman who looked like a bundle of duds was asleep in the corner, while next to her sat the young one as wide awake as himself, her fingers picking at each other as if she were plucking a chicken. Mother, indeed! There was no resemblance whatever between this nerve-racked creature and the child; yet he had no doubt but that she was Bella's mother and would fight for the custody of her, and he was powerless to stop it.

Had his son been as bad to her as she had said? . . . The answer came clear in his mind. Yes, his son had been spoiled by his mother from the day he was born. He had only to cry to get what he wanted. He himself had thought to erase the boy's selfishness with the rod and the Bible, but he had failed. Given the chance again, he told himself that he wouldn't fail. It had come to him over the past few weeks while the child had been in this house with him that there were other ways of disciplining youth besides the threat of the birch or the Bible.

He himself should be making use of the Bible at this moment – he should be praying to God for her safety. But God seemed very far away. God seemed to have joined all his neighbours, all the villagers, everyone he knew, because he was a man alone, a man who wanted to be alone . . . no, had wanted to be alone, because now he wanted to be alone no longer. Since that chit of a child had come into his life it was as if she had driven a wedge between his ribs and her warmth had seeped through to his heart. There was a feeling in him now that he had never experienced before; it was such that it was having the power to melt the iron bands that had held together his dogmatic opinions, his bigotry, his cutting and hurtful tongue that he had always thought of simply as forthright speech. It was such a feeling that it was depleting him entirely of the character he had built up over the years, and at present he had no weapon with which to fight it. He saw himself at this time more than ever as a man alone.

It was at the point when his thoughts turned towards God and he was about to bargain with Him, saying, 'Bring her back, Lord, and I'll let her go to her mother without a word of protest,' that he heard a scrambling of footsteps across the yard. The whole room sprang to life as the

165

door burst open and before his amazed gaze three figures, two almost coal black, tumbled into the room.

There was a moment of silence, deep amazed silence; then everyone outdid the other in shouting.

'Oh, John! John!'

'It's the bairn.'

'Where in the name of God . . .!'

'Oh, Bella! Bella!'

'Glory be to God . . . but did you ever . . .?'

'Oh, Mrs Golightly . . . Oh, Mrs Golightly.'

Joseph was the only one to have made no comment at all, but now, walking like a man in a dream towards the three figures, he gently pushed the young woman aside and, thrusting out his arms, lifted Bella into them, and she, flinging her arms around his neck, cried, 'Granda! Oh, Granda! Granda!'

'Listen! Listen, everybody. Shut up, will you!' John's last words were almost a scream and they silenced the whole company. 'Dad' – he turned to his father – 'look sharp. He's still in the cellar.'

'Who? What you talking about, boy?'

'Sir Geoffrey Cotton-Bailey, the man they kidnapped. She was right, she was right all along. Mr Aimsford, he's . . . he's a gangster, and they're going to get him away tonight, Mr . . . Mr Bailey. He's too weak, he couldn't get through the coal hole with us.'

'Which coal hole? What are you talking about, lad?'

John turned on Dave Seaton, crying, 'The coal hole at the manor.' He thumbed towards the wall. 'It's next to a secret cellar where we've been kept.'

166

'Name of God!' Jack Pollock gave a small laugh. 'Kidnapping! Secret cellars! From the look of you now, it strikes me you've been with Pat Picton here at his charcoal burning.'

'He ain't, and he's speaking the truth.' Pat's rough voice silenced Mr Pollock. 'An' if you want to catch those fellows, you'd better stop your yappin' an' get a move on. An' don't forget to take a ladder with ya.'

'He's right, he's right. They'll have Mr Bailey on their boat if you don't look sharp.' Bella had swung around within the circle of her grandfather's arms, and now quickly turning towards him again, she cupped his hairy face in her hands, saying, 'Go and get him, Granda, please. I told him you would. I told him you'd go back and get him.'

Joseph Dodd stared into the black smudged face. Then with a quick movement he pressed her to him before putting her down on the floor. Now with a 'Come on! Let's see what this is about,' he went towards the door. But the two boys were already through it, with Harry Thompson close on their heels.

In the yard Joseph kept pace with Harry, while Jack Pollock and Dave Seaton brought up the rear, but hesitantly it would seem, for they still couldn't take in what they had heard. 'That couldn't happen in this village, kidnapping. That's something you read about in newspapers.' And Jack Pollock said as much to Pat as the young lad pulled a ladder away from a stacked pile of osiers. 'True, is it? Not havin' us on?'

'Don't be so stupid.'

'Mind your blasted cheek, you young 'un.'

167

'Well, don't ask for it then . . . "Havin' us on?"
ya said. I got them out of the coal cellar, didn't I?'

'Shut your noise, you two.' It was Joseph's
voice hissing at them. 'And put that torch out,
Seaton.'

'It's black dark. I won't be able to see a stone.'

'Put your finger in your eye and make a star-
light.' As Jack Pollock's quip brought a sharp
rejoinder from Harry, Joseph's voice hissed,
'This is no laughin' matter.'

'Why not? The bairns are safe.'

'Well, you're not deaf, are you? You heard what
the lad said about the man back there.'

'Aye; aye, I did. An' I'll believe I'm lookin' at a
kidnapped man when I see him.'

'Well, that won't be long then, Mr Pollock. At
least, I hope so,' said John now. 'That's if they
haven't already got him out of the cellar and
away to the coast. And another thing, I think it
would work better, Dad, if you and Mr Pollock
and Mr Seaton went to the front door and
knocked and pretended you were enquiring after
us, for then if they haven't already gone down
into the cellar that would divert them a bit and
give us time to get Mr Bailey up. Mr Dodd and
Pat and me'll manage that.'

'Yes, yes, it seems a good idea, John. We'll do
that.'

'If you are going to do anything but talk, you'd
better get a move on, and you'd better hang on to
each other and tread quietly as we go through my
wood,' growled Joseph.

'Through your wood?'

'Yes, through my wood; an' as I said, quietly.'

'Oh, we'll tread quietly, all right. We could
teach you a thing or two, Dodd, in that way,

couldn't we, Jack?' It seemed that Mr Seaton was bent on taking the matter lightly. 'There's one or two pheasants haven't known which donkey kicked 'em . . .'

'Hold your tongue, man.' The tone of Joseph's voice had the power to silence them all; and then they were moving cautiously but swiftly along by the guide rope.

They all stopped as someone slipped and dislodged the stones as he was going over the broken wall, and when Mr Pollock's oath proclaimed who it was they remained silent, listening.

When finally they had crawled through the base of the fir hedge, they stood in a line on the grass verge and gazed up the empty drive towards the house. After the darkness of the wood it looked as if the whole place were bathed in dim moonlight.

'There's no need for caution now,' Harry whispered. 'We'll walk boldly to the front door, and once it's open we'll get inside. You're pretty good with your fists, aren't you, Dave?'

'Try me.' Dave Seaton seemed to be more in his element now.

'You all right, John?' Harry was speaking quietly to his son and John said, 'Yes, Dad.'

'Good. Then let's away.'

The six of them moved noisily onto the gravel drive, purposely walking more heavily than was necessary, but as soon as they were opposite the front door John tugged at Joseph's sleeve. Jerking the end of the ladder he was holding as a signal to Pat at the other end, they set off at a run around to the far side of the house.

When they came to the coal hatch it was Pat who with one heave lifted up the iron lid; and then both he and John glanced at each other in consternation as they heard the sound of scuffling and voices coming from below them.

'They've got him! They've got him!' John flashed his torch down into the hole, but before he could make any further comment the torch was grabbed from his hand and he was pushed aside by Joseph, who, after one swift glance down into the coal house, shouted, 'Give us the ladder here!'

Within seconds John and Pat had the ladder upright and were pushing it downwards. Before it reached the bottom the futility of this manoeuvre made itself evident to John, and now he cried, 'It's right across the hole. We couldn't get down there.'

'Begod! You're right, boy.' Joseph was now on his feet. 'Come on.' Like a young man, he spurted forward to the front of the house again, with John and Pat at his heels. When they reached the door they found it open, and the sound of further scuffling came to them.

There was a light in the hall that showed a broad staircase branching off from both sides into a gallery. John had only time to take in the fact that, apart from a couple of chairs and an old trunk, there was no furniture in the hall; the next minute he was running behind Joseph into a large room. This, too, was furnished sparsely, but he noticed that it held a couch, some easy chairs, and a table, and it was towards the table that he now ran to where Jack Pollock and Dave Seaton were struggling with a man on the floor. It was Jack Pollock who, looking up at Joseph, gasped, 'Tie his legs, will you, with anything . . . your tie . . . your muffler.'

'Where's my dad?'

170

Before Jack Pollock or Dave Seaton, who had tied the man's hands behind him, could give John a reply, their attention and that of Joseph and Pat and of John himself was brought towards the fireplace, where a long frame that had once held a portrait and was attached to a wall seemed to be slowly moving towards them. As John was about to run towards it he was brought to a halt by Joseph's reaching out and gripping his coat, then tugging him backwards.

Joseph's position on the floor was almost opposite the picture frame and he had seen what neither John nor Pat nor the two men who were holding down Dick Riley had seen, and that was Harry stepping backwards into the room.

When a voice came to them, saying, 'Put them up further ... further!' Harry came full into view, his hands above his head, and facing him was Mr Aimsford, a revolver held steadily in his hand.

What prompted John to move swiftly towards the fireplace and pull Pat with him as he went he could never explain, nor that they should stand crouched in the corner between the end of the fireplace and the side of the swivelled picture frame. Perhaps it was the fact that for a moment Mr Aimsford had his back to them; that was before he motioned Joseph, Jack Pollock, and Dave Seaton to join his father at the other side of the opening.

It was when Joseph refused to move that Harry said quietly, 'Don't attempt it, Joseph, he means business.'

'You're a wise man, Mr Thompson.' Aimsford's voice had a sarcastic note to it, and when he added, 'If you had kept off the drink, I

171

am sure you would have been a successful man,'
John's head drooped towards his chest for a
moment. But the next second it was brought up
by the sound of scuffling feet just beyond the
panel. There came into his view the stumbling
form of Sir Geoffrey, again gagged and his hands
tied behind his back. That he had put up a fight
was evident from the blood running down the
side of his face.

'How do you hope to get away with this?' It
was Joseph's voice, like a growl, speaking now,
and the answer came quietly, which made it all
the more ominous: 'Leave that to me, Mr Dodd.
You and your friends have only slightly impeded
our departure. As you will note, physically we are
equal, but mentally we, I should say, are way
ahead. In my short sojourn among you I have
found you all very stupid; with perhaps one
exception, the child, the bright child, your granddaughter, Mr Dodd. It's a pity your wits aren't as
sharp as hers, for she saw more through her
blindness than you all did with your eyes. But
now I'm wasting time, come!'

As John and Pat stood breathing into each other's face, the swivelling movements of their eyes
and almost imperceptible movements of their
heads indicated to each other what they were
about to do.

John mouthed towards Pat the word 'Tackle',
and demonstrated further by thrusting his hand
out in a grabbing motion. After a second Pat
nodded at him.

Aimsford had now taken two side steps further
into the room, and with his left hand he motioned
towards the men who were holding Sir Geoffrey
and from them to the writhing figure on the floor,

172

saying harshly, 'Don't stand there holding him up, put him down and unloosen Dick. And now you ... gentlemen, kindly walk this way and down the steps and into the room that our friend' – he indicated Sir Geoffrey – 'and your children have so lately vacated. And don't imagine that you will make your escape as they did by the coal hatch. There's an iron bar that goes across there and we won't forget to put it into place before we leave ... Come on now, move!' Aimsford's voice changed again. 'I'm not playing games. I've used this before and to effect. It's in for a penny, in for a pound. And when they find you, which they undoubtedly will with the help of the children, it would be nicer all round if there weren't a couple of dead bodies among you; so come on, no playing about, *move!*'

Perhaps it was the gasp that John gave as both he and Pat sprang forward that made Aimsford spin around, but as the two figures hurled themselves on him he was borne backwards, and the next minute John found himself in what appeared to be the midst of a rugby scrum. There were bodies all over him, legs and arms flailing. He didn't know who was friend or who was foe; there was only one thing certain – he was still clinging on to Aimsford.

When the fist caught him on the side of the jaw, he had the sensation of being lifted upwards from the floor and sent ceilingward; and the strange thing was he couldn't remember coming down.

10

'It's all right, it's all right, he's coming round.'

'Oh . . . my head . . . my head.'

'It's all right, it's all right.'

'Put me down, I want to get on . . . onto the floor.'

Somebody laughed, then a voice said, 'That's your trouble, you've been too long on the floor, and had too much weight on you. Come on, come on, drink this.'

John blinked his eyes and looked up into a sea of faces all floating around him. The doctor from the village, his father, Mr Dodd, Mrs Campbell, Pat. He put his hand out and Pat gripped it; and now he muttered, 'Wha . . . what . . . what happened? Oh, my head!' He went to rise, but someone pressed him back and he looked up at them, saying, 'They . . . they got away?'

'Not on your nelly.' It was Pat's rough, laughing voice, and now John blinked towards him as he said, 'No?'

'Lie still.' It was the doctor again.

Then Harry was bending over him. 'Don't worry, we've got them all. They're on their way now to where they won't cause any mischief for some time.'

'Sir . . . Sir Geoffrey?'

'Mister's here.'

At the sound of Bella's voice he again attempted to sit up, but found the effort too much and could only turn his head in her direction. He saw her sitting by the big chair, and in it, leaning back, his eyes closed, was Sir Geoffrey.

'Is he all right?'

'Yes, yes.' Harry's tone was soothing. 'But he's very tired and weak, and the loss of blood hasn't helped.'

As he went to close his eyes Bella's voice came to him again, with a quiver in it now, saying softly, 'He never asked after me, did he? I was the only one he missed out.'

'Aw, child, he knew you were safe and sound,' said Mrs Golightly now. Then her voice rising to a sharp crescendo, she cried, 'Aw, no, no, hinny; now don't start that. Aw, no! Now stop it. Stop it! You're not to cry.'

But the admonition could have been a signal for Bella to let go, for now her high-pitched wail filled the room.

'It's all right, it's all right, dear. Come along now, stop crying.'

But Mrs Campbell's voice seemed only to aggravate the sound, and Joseph, going quickly towards Bella, tugged her away from her mother's arms and into his own. When her head was buried in his shoulder he said, 'What's all this? Come on, come on now. After all you've been through, and not a wet eye, to make a show like this! Doesn't make sense. Come on, come on.'

'It's likely a reaction. She'll be all right. It's better to let her cry.'

The doctor meant his words to be soothing but Mrs Golightly soon disabused his suggestion as she shouted above the noise of Bella's weeping,

'You know nowt about it, at least not yet. I've known this to go on for two solid days. Last time she had to be put to sleep. She rarely cries, but when she does she does it properly, let me tell you. She made herself so ill she was in bed for a week once with it.'

'Well, in that case forewarned is forearmed. We'll have to see she doesn't cry for two days, won't we?'

It was apparent from his voice that the doctor hadn't taken to Mrs Golightly, and now he added, 'The best place for her is bed, and I'll come and see her in a minute.'

Joseph said nothing as he walked through the crowded room and went to mount the stairs, and when he saw that the child's mother and Mrs Golightly were following him, he looked over his shoulder and almost growled at them, 'I'll see to her.'

'With her mother's help you will.'

Joseph now looked past Mrs Campbell and down onto the broad wrinkled face, and all he said was, '*Women!*' but it expressed more than a battery of words.

Bella knew that she should stop crying. She tried her best, she even said to herself, 'Stop it, will you! Stop it. Everything's all right, so stop it.' But she couldn't stop it. She was experiencing sorrow that had its source somewhere deep within her, and as it spurted up through her body and spilled out of her eyes, her nose, and her mouth, it bore on its surface, like boats on a river in spate, things forgotten, things that she had consciously buried, like the dim memory of her da hitting a woman, bashing his fists into her face,

176

then kicking her when she lay on the floor. Then this picture was swamped by the feeling of being lost. Although she was in a room and she could make out the objects as through a mist, she knew she was lost and there was nobody to come and find her because her da had gone out and left her.

Into the scenes flooding up, her grandfather's voice came, shouting, 'Don't fuss, woman! If you're going to get her things off, get them off. Stop your chatter!' Then Mrs Golightly's voice, which made her want to laugh through her tears, as she shouted back at her granda: 'And you shut your whist, man, for if you don't I'm as likely to take your clothes off an' take me hand to your backside, 'cos you're showing no more sense than a bairn.' But she didn't laugh.

The picture in her mind now was of a great roaring of traffic and people yelling and a man picking her up and running with her and voices all around shouting, 'She could have been run over. Fancy letting a blind child out by herself.' She had struggled and pushed at the hands, then shouted at them, 'I can go about by meself. I just took the wrong crossin'.'

It was when she felt a sharp prick in her arm that the waves in her mind washed up the worst picture of all. It was when they told her that her father was dead. She had been lost a long time then because she hadn't anybody, not even Mrs Golightly, and not even Miss Talbot, but a strange woman from the centre. She had been frightened . . . and then she had met her granda.

'Gran . . . da! Gran . . . da!'

'Yes, I'm here, hinny.'

She felt him gripping her hands but she still couldn't stop crying; and if anybody could make

177

her stop crying it was her granda, because he was the only one in the world belonging to her. . . What was that? There were no other women in the room but Mrs Campbell and Mrs Golightly, and Mrs Golightly had said, 'Let her mother undress her.'

She was dreaming. She was dreaming. She hadn't a mother. Never had a mother. But she didn't mind as long as she had a granda.

11

She wished they would let her wake up. Why
couldn't they let her wake up properly? She had
stopped crying, oh, a long, long time ago ...
Well, it seemed a long time ago. Was it yesterday,
or the day before, or the day before that? What
day was it?

She asked someone the day and they said it
was Tuesday.

Silly, it couldn't be Tuesday. Somewhere in her
mind everything was clear, that is, everything
that had happened on Friday. At least it was
clear in bits, if they wouldn't keep pushing her off
to sleep again. 'Drink this,' they said. 'Drink
this.' And off she would go, floating away while
voices bobbed up all around her, the doctor's
voice saying, 'The best thing for her. Her mind's
too active by far.'

Her mind too active by far – what did he
mean? Was he going to stop her thinking? Could
he stop her thinking? She wanted to keep awake
to know what was happening. She wanted to keep
awake to talk to John. And yes, Pat, too. Funny,
but she liked Pat. As she had heard someone say,
'If it hadn't been for Pat, they would have had a
poor lookout.' Who had said that? The mister?
... Yes, the sir. He must have been up in her

179

bedroom when they were pushing her off to sleep again. Oh, she wanted to talk, she wanted to hear all the news. And there was something very important she wanted to ask. It was about Mrs Campbell. Mrs Campbell seemed to be always near her, and the word 'mother' had cropped up a number of times. She must have been dreaming that part.

When she finally woke up, really woke up, she lay with her eyes closed, thinking. Her mind was quite clear. She knew where she was. She was in her own bedroom, in her own bed, in her granda's house. But was she really Bella, Bella Dodd? Was she really blind, because for a long time now she had seemed to be seeing people? Well, she always saw people in her dreams. She could see in her dreams. What she must do now was to open her eyes and find out if she was really Bella Dodd.

Slowly she lifted her lids, and when they revealed no light she lay perfectly still. Yes, yes, she was really Bella Dodd.

She lay for some time quite still and then she became aware of the voices, and as she did so she knew that it was the voices that had woken her up. They had been rising and falling for a long time. It seemed as if they were coming from under the bed. This thought made her smile because in a way they *were* coming from under the bed, from the room downstairs, and her sharp ears picked up the fact that because they were clearer than usual her bedroom door must be open.

She sat up and turned her head towards the window, and when the blackness around her was lightened slightly she knew it was daytime and that the sun was shining.

180

She pushed the bedclothes back and swung her feet over the side of the bed, and when they touched the rug she inclined her head downwards. It was a different rug, soft, thick, thick enough for her toes to grip.

She walked off the rug and onto the bare boards and was bending to grope for her slippers when her hands were stayed by the sound of her grandfather's voice. It sounded strange, because it was quiet; yet there was bitterness threading it as he said, 'You've got it all worked out between you, haven't you? You, Harry Thompson, so you tell me, are going to start a new life for yourself with my late son's wife, and she, out of gratitude, is going to give Mrs Golightly there her cottage. Very nice, very nice for Mrs Golightly. . .'

'Now, you look here!'

'No, no, you look here, Mrs Golightly. I've listened to you all talking for days now. You've got it all arranged. Before she takes up her abode among you, you're going to allow her a holiday on Sir Geoffrey's yacht, together with John and young Pat and, if Pat gets his own way, his brother Gerry. I'm not saying it won't be nice for them, nor that it's as little as Sir Geoffrey can do, seeing that amongst them they've saved his neck and half a million ransom. But there's two people you've left out of all this, you've not given a thought to, not really: first there's her and then there's me. Well, say you wipe me off the slate, what about her? Have any of you thought of waiting until she can speak for herself, until she can say what she wants to do, because if I know anything about her she won't be backward in coming forward in speaking the truth?'

Bella stood on the landing, pulling her dressing

gown around her. After a moment she became still and pressed her hand against the wall. As her granda had said, they had it all cut and dried. But what did she want to do? Who did she want to live with? One thing was clear to her now and that was Mrs Campbell was her mother. She didn't know how it had come about, only that she seemed to have known it from the first time they touched hands. She liked Mrs Campbell. Oh yes, she did, she did. And she liked Mr Thompson. Oh yes, he was a lovely man. And John. Oh well, she couldn't explain what she felt about John.

She knew that she was standing at the top of the stairs and that from the silence that had now settled on the room they were aware of her presence.

Before she was halfway down the stairs the voices surrounded her.

'Oh! My dear, you'll catch cold.'

'How do you feel?'

'There you are then, on your pins again.' That was Mrs Golightly.

From a certain reserve in their voices she knew they were aware that she was aware of all that had been said.

'Here, sit down. Let me fasten your dressing gown.' It was her mother's voice, her mother's hands touching her, and she smiled upwards towards her.

Then John, punching her gently on the shoulder, said, 'Hello, you.'

'Hello, you, yourself.' Their short laughs met and mingled.

'How you feelin'?' It was Pat's voice.

'All right, Pat, fine.'

182

'You look as good as new, fightin' fit.'

'You've been in the papers, you know that?'

'Have I, Mr Thompson?'

'They'll be pinning medals on you when you go into the town.'

She laughed outright now, then moved her head from side to side as if looking for someone.

The only one who hadn't spoken to her was her granda, but she knew he was there.

When the room became quiet again, the silence yelled at her and after a moment she was forced to speak. What she said was, 'I heard what you were sayin' a bit back.'

'Trust you.' John's embarrassed laugh came at her and she flapped her hand towards him. Then linking her fingers together, she laid her hands on her lap and she made a little rocking movement before asking, 'Are ... are you going to marry Mrs Campbell, Mr Thompson?'

'... Yes, my dear. And I don't know whether you have taken it in but ... but Mrs Campbell is really your mother. Do you know that?'

'Yes, yes, I do.'

'Aren't you glad that ... that you have a mother?'

'Oh yes, yes.'

Her hands were lifted from her lap and she knew that Mrs Campbell was holding them and that she lifted her head up to her as she said, 'Oh, my dear, my dear.'

All of a sudden she felt sorry for Mrs Campbell, very sorry. She wanted to pat her hands, or her shoulder, or her cheek to comfort her, but she knew what she couldn't do as yet was to put her arms around her; she was too new a mother. She had never thought of a mother in her life; a father,

183

yes, or a grandfather, oh yes, but never a mother. Still it was very nice to have a mother, if only . . .

Mr Thompson was now speaking, saying quietly, 'You'll like living along the road with us, and you'll have John to fight with all the time.' He gave a little laugh, but she made no effort to join in. Now drawing her hands gently from those of her mother, she slipped off the chair and said quietly, 'Granda!'

'Aye.' His voice came from somewhere near the door and she knew that the way across the room was open to her, and slowly she walked towards him. When her fingers touched his rough jacket, she put her arms upwards and the next minute she was pressed close to him and his whiskery lips were kissing her cheek.

'Aw, Granda! Granda!'

'It's all right, hinny, it's all right.'

'Aw, Granda!'

'Oh, my God! Don't you start your cryin' again else we'll all be done for, drowned.'

'Who's going to cry?' She turned her head in Mrs Golightly's direction. 'I'm not gonna cry. I've got nothin' to cry about.'

'Well, that's something to thank God for.' Mrs Golightly's quip didn't raise even a titter because everyone seemed to be waiting for Bella to speak. With one arm hugging her grandfather's neck, she turned her face towards him and said, quite simply, 'I want to live here with me granda. I won't be happy anywhere else except with him.'

She felt the quiver pass through her grandfather's body, and when he made a strange sound in his throat she put her other hand on his stubbly cheek.

184

'It's impossible. Who'd look after you?' It was her mother speaking in broken tones now.

'He's looked after me all the holidays, an' I can look after meself a lot.'

'But . . . but this house is no place . . .'

'It doesn't matter about the house. Anyway, it could be made nice, couldn't it, Granda?'

She didn't wait for him to answer her for she knew that for once he would be unable to speak, he was trembling so much. Instead she turned her attention to Mrs Golightly as she said, 'You've told me yourself, haven't you, Mrs Golightly, many a time, it isn't houses that matter, it's people?'

And for once Mrs Golightly failed to reply also. Again there came on the kitchen the silence, the loud silence, and it was John who broke it now, saying quietly, 'She's right; it's people not houses that matter. Anyway, we're all close together and we can see to her.'

She knew by the way his voice was swinging away from her that he was turning his head in different directions, and he went on, 'We can all help Mr Dodd; that's . . . that's if he wants any help.'

There was a pause before Harry said quietly, 'Yes, you're right, boy, you're right.'

Bella felt her grandfather press her tightly towards him for a moment before quickly putting her to the ground, and she wasn't surprised at all when she heard him go out of the door and she was left standing alone. She knew they were all at the other end of the room, Mrs Golightly, Pat, Mr Thompson, her mother, and John, and quickly she said to them, 'You've all got somebody and he's got nobody, like I once had, nobody, and it's an

185

awful feelin', and as John said, we'll all live together, like on the same street.'

As she heard someone sobbing she moved quickly in that direction. Now she did put her arms around her mother, and said softly, 'Aw, don't . . . don't you cry, 'cos I'll be with you a lot. I'll . . . I'll want you to help me put the house straight 'cos it's in a bit of a mess, isn't it? I knew it was in a bit of a mess the first day I came into it. I could tell by the smell, but . . . but I had to make on. But we could make it nice, couldn't we?'

'Oh, my dear, my dear.' Again there was silence until her mother murmured, 'Yes, yes, I suppose we could make it nice; between us we could make it nice.'

Slowly Bella now put her face forward, pursed her lips, and kissed her mother. For the first time she kissed her mother. Then, after a moment during which she was held tightly, she disengaged herself and, turning towards John, she said brightly, 'Was it right what I heard, have we been invited onto a boat?'

'Yes, we have, Pat here, and you and me. But . . . but Pat says he won't go unless Gerry's invited too.'

'Oh!' She now turned in the direction where she thought Pat was standing and said, 'He's a bit of a stinker, your brother, isn't he? But I suppose we could manage him atween us. An' if he plays up we could chuck him overboard.'

'Aye, that's an idea. I've thought about doin' that meself before now.'

'Here, stop your chatter.' It was Mrs Golightly who had hold of her arm now, pulling her forward, while she said, 'Before you start making your arrangements, go out into the yard there an' ask

186

that old tyrant if it's all right for you to go on the boat. You're goin' in any case, but it's courtesy like, an' it'll make him think he's still boss. He's standin' near the gate. Pull your dressing gown around you. There you are.'

Her arms flew up and around Mrs Golightly's neck, and as she hugged her she cried, 'Oh, you're lovely, Mrs Golightly! You're lovely. Everybody thought you were just 'magination, but you're not, are you?'

'No, begod! I'm not 'magination.' Mrs Golightly had pulled open the door now and as she pushed Bella gently forward, she said, 'And that old pain in the neck will be made to realize I'm not 'magination if I know anything about it come the future; an' you can go and tell him what I said.'

Bella's hands spread out before her and, laughing inside herself, she walked slowly and steadily towards the gate. When she touched his coat his arm came around her shoulders and he pressed her to his side. Then he asked grimly, 'Now what was that one saying to you?' And after a moment she answered in a casual tone, 'Oh, she was just sayin' that at bottom you were a fine enough man, a bit sharp in the temper, but nevertheless good, and she would do all she could to . . . to help you in the future. You . . . you have only to ask.'

It was she now who pressed her head tightly against his thigh as for the first time she heard him laugh as he said, 'Tell that to the marines, or better still, go back there an' tell it to Mrs Golightly. Tell her what she's supposed to have said about me, and she'll have a fit and die of it . . . an' the sooner the better.'

187

'Aw, Granda! Granda, that's funny.' She was laughing with him . . . spluttering.

'Bella, Bella' – his hand was on her hair – 'we'll have a grand life of it together, you an' me. I'll see you want for nothing.' He bent towards her. 'If you want anything, you ask me. Understand? You ask me.'

'Yes, Granda, yes . . . Granda?'

'Aye?'

'Will you call me Joy?'

'Joy? No, begod! I won't.' The softness was gone. 'Bella you are, and Bella you'll remain. It's a fine, sturdy name. Joy, indeed . . . Come on! Get yourself in before you catch your death. Joy. Never heard of such a name. And why did that lot let you out of doors and you just out of a warm bed? Things are going to change around here from now on, I can tell you. Come on, inside you get.'

'Granda, when are we gonna get that dog?'

'Oh, we'll talk about that some other time. Enough is enough.'

'. . . Oh, well, all right. But until we do I'll keep Gip. Come on, Gip! Come on, boy, come on, run.'

'. . . Bella! *Bella!*

. . . Bella! *Bella!*

. . . Bella! *Bella!*'

And ignoring her grandfather's voice, she ran.

'Oh, there you are, Mrs Golightly. Granda says he'll be glad of your help and thanks very much.'

Bella knew that Mrs Golightly was leaning against the door and that her whole body was wobbling, because the door was wobbling.

Everything was lovely, bright and shining, inside her head.

THE END